...rience, like reading someone's
...honest diary.' *Meanjin*

'*My Hundred Lovers* is, in the end, a genuinely life-affirming book. Yes, it's true that "every day unique in its details (is) already passing, vanishing, like breath", but what a privilege to be able to enjoy this day, this experience, this lover right now.' *The Australian*

'The pleasures of bathing, cycling, Paris and song are threaded through memories of unrequited love, unrealised longing and lovers.' *Canberra Times*

'*My Hundred Lovers* is an original imagining of one woman's waning flesh and the vibrant imprint of a life it still holds.' *The Age*

'Johnson's prose is lucid and poetic, beautifully crafted.' *Brisbane News*

'The writing has a candour and physical honesty about how memory lodges in the body as potently as in the mind.' *Better Homes and Gardens*

Praise for *The Broken Book*

'Both very Australian and resoundingly international, *The Broken Book* confirms Johnson's status as one of the finest Australian writers . . . fiercely beautiful.' *The Australian*

'A bold narrative, in which we're constantly reminded by the quality of her prose that this is an imaginative work . . . It's a kaleidoscope of memory, jagged and disordered as the artist's tragic life.' *Canberra Times*

'An astonishing novel . . . a jewel of a book.' *Vogue Australia*

'*The Broken Book* is wonderfully rich, complex and compelling. Susan Johnson has created an audacious and original novel with an awe-inspiring ability to explore emotional truths.' *Daily Advertiser*

Praise for *Life in Seven Mistakes*

'Feeling, insight, rambunctious wit.' *New York Times Book Review*

'She has a knack for presenting what can be unbearable in reality, of rendering it on the page with tremendous heart.' *Sydney Morning Herald*

Susan Johnson was shortlisted for the 1991 Victorian Premier's Literary Award for her novel *Flying Lessons*, shortlisted for the 1994 National Book Council's Banjo Award for the novel *A Big Life* and shortlisted for the National Biography Award 2000 for her memoir *A Better Woman*. Her other books include *Hungry Ghosts*, *Messages from Chaos*, *Women Love Sex* (editor and contributor) and *Life in Seven Mistakes*. *The Broken Book* was shortlisted for the 2005 Nita B Kibble Award; the Best Fiction Book section of the Queensland Premier's Literary Award; the Westfield/Waverley Library Literary Award; and the Australian Literary Society Gold Medal Award for an Outstanding Australian Literary Work.

In 2010 she returned from ten years in London to live in Brisbane. She is a feature writer at *Qweekend* magazine, and lives with her teenage sons in Kangaroo Point.

ALSO BY SUSAN JOHNSON

My Hundred Lovers

Susan Johnson

ALLEN&UNWIN

SYDNEY • MELBOURNE • AUCKLAND • LONDON

This edition published in 2013
First published in 2012

Allen & Unwin
83 Alexander Street
Crows Nest NSW 2065
Australia
Phone: (61 2) 8425 0100
Email: info@allenandunwin.com
Web: www.allenandunwin.com

Cataloguing-in-Publication details are available
from the National Library of Australia
www.trove.nla.gov.au

ISBN 978 1 74331 569 9

Design by Sandy Cull, gogoGingko
Typeset in 12.5/17 Mrs Eaves OT CE by Bookhouse, Sydney
Printed and bound in Australia by Griffin Press

10 9 8 7 6 5 4 3 2

For Simone Bocognano, with love and admiration

My lovers suffocate me,

Crowding my lips, thick in the pores of my skin,

Jostling me through streets and public halls, coming naked to me at night,

Crying by day, Ahoy! from the rocks of the river, swinging and

chirping over my head,

Calling my name from flower-beds, vines, tangled underbrush,

Lighting on every moment of my life . . .

WALT WHITMAN,
'Song of Myself'

If the body is not a *thing*, it is a situation . . .

it is the instrument of our grasp upon the world.

SIMONE DE BEAUVOIR,
The Second Sex

Gods

ROMANCE BETWEEN THE AVERAGE COUPLE dies two years, six months and twenty-five days into marriage.

This regrettable statistic is based on a 2009 survey into the hearts of three thousand English couples.

Romance was alive and well one night in 1959 in Sydney, Australia, when my father's penis first slipped inside my mother. In the back seat of his blue Humber my mother was losing her bra, her girdle, her girlish breath and it was not yet clear what she was gaining.

Romance between this average couple died on a bright winter's morning some eight months, two days and ten hours into their marriage, when my mother caught my father kissing the prettiest of his secretaries while simultaneously attempting to unhook her underwire bra. My mother had thought to surprise my father with an unannounced visit to his office but it was she who got the surprise.

She was eight months pregnant, no good at forgiveness, and she was trapped. Trapped in a marriage, trapped in her body, trapped, trapped, trapped.

My father, David, was fatal to women. Technically he should not have been handsome, in that he possessed somewhat large crooked teeth and a lopsided smile, yet somehow his hooded grey eyes and his slow easy grace made you think he was good-looking. He was tall and big-shouldered, with a kind of drawling sensuality about his person which more properly belonged to the bedroom. He had very sensual lips.

My father was what is called a seductive father.

My father was a suburban sex god.

THREE

Incarnation

HERE IS THE WARMTH, NO, the heat, the pulse of blood. Here is the collision—of circumstances, of DNA, of myriad impossible, unutterable hopes.

Everything is coming together: the past, the future, memory, forgetting. A circumstantial joining, a burst, a throb.

Created.

Soon the glistening chambers of the heart, the ductless glands, the nuchal membrane, as transparent as vapour. The coiled ear getting ready to hear, the pearly eye to see.

Soon the first sound: the beats of my mother's heart.

All the world's wonders, arriving!

Some time later, I am born.

I feel the embrace of arms, of hands, of soft materials against my skin. For the first time I feel the roll of the nipple against my tongue. Sweet milk floods my mouth, a trace of salt. My eyes are closed and there is the smell of the first woman, my mother, a musky animal smell that comes from under my mother's arms, from her breath, from between her legs. My first love.

Can a body, confined to the modest compass of an ordinary skin, tell you everything? In the fifty years between my birth and now I have experienced no wars or plagues. I was born into the western world in a rare, safe moment of history. I stand here unembroidered by historical grandeur or incident.

I am an ordinary citizen of the sated world and nothing exceptional has ever happened to me, save the commonplace and extraordinary fact that, like you, I was born, I was born, I was born.

In the last few years I have felt myself to be increasingly laden with memories, as if the past is more weighted, more densely textured, than the present.

On certain days I feel as if I might walk straight from the present into the past, so near does it feel to me. I remember the smell of rooms, and the way my legs looked on a summer morning long ago when Nina Payne and I lay on our backs and put our legs up against the wall of our house. I remember the feel of the hot wall against my heels and noticing for the first time that my legs were hairy. There was the rattle and hiss of cicadas in the trees above us and the sickly smell of frangipani mixed with fragrant clouds of jasmine. The jasmine ran up the wall, spilling above our legs in white frothy profusion.

The topography of this long-ago moment is readily available to me, the exact shape of it, the colour and taste: it is the present moment which is dissolving.

In the months leading up to my fiftieth birthday I observed the first tentative signs of life's waning. The blood which had flowed from me month after month for almost forty years began to flow fitfully. At the same time the face I had worn all my adult life began to change into the face of someone else. I was forced to understand that there was a direct link between the body's hormonal succulence and the succulence of youth.

I was drying up.

My body was in the thrilling first flush of its death throes.

I have witnessed my grandmother's waning, and my mother's, both reduced to pure body in the end. In their last years and months each became a body without a mind to comprehend it, fleshy vessels for ingesting and excreting, since everything their once-teeming brains knew had vanished. They lived without cognitive maps, living on in their bodies without memories. As I watched the departure of my mother, I began to consider exactly what is essential in a human being. It seemed to me that once a person forgets the music she has heard, the places she has seen and the faces she has known, she becomes like a person in a photograph, resembling herself but locked in a moment that has passed. And once a person loses the memory of desire, the ability to understand the difference between want and its absence, between happiness and unhappiness, the most fundamental apprehension of existence is lost.

I understood then that a person estranged from the body's meaning has slipped the bonds of herself. Disembodied from the memory of touch and want, from the remembered breaths of lovers and children and friends, a self is vanished. If it is true that we are more than our bodies, it is also true that without an apprehension of our bodies we disappear. Who was that person shuffling along a nursing-home corridor to the table and then back to the bed? It was my mother's body, but was it my mother?

Half a century has passed since I entered the world through that now-perished body.

A human lifespan is less than a thousand months long.

I find myself gripped by an urge to tidy up, to sort through my body's memories, a curator arranging artefacts in a museum. I have lived my way into a time in which my body has its own archaeology.

I am in a fever to outrun myself, to be first to reach the ribbon, before my body forgets what it means to run.

I look behind me and remember a prickle upon the skin, a swoop of pain, the rush of blood to the face when I saw a man with whom I was newly in love. I remember the way my stomach lurched whenever I saw him, as if I were travelling too fast in a car over an unexpected hill. My heart has a memory.

I recall the sensation of love in the rhythm my grandmother, Nana Elsie, tapped out upon my back when she was cradling me, long after I was a child, when I was a big, ungainly adolescent girl with hormonal pimples. Her love singled me out, filled me with a swelling feeling of joy, as if inoculating me against the grief and pain to come.

I remember a peach I once ate in a garden in France, sitting next to my new husband. The sweetness of the peach seemed to match the sweetness at the heart of the world. At that moment I believed I would never again feel contingent, or estranged from sweetness.

I remember the hot swell of newborn flesh against my breast as I suckled my son, and how there was nothing but repletion in his fresh eyes.

And who but me will remember these things? Who but me experienced them with her ten fingers and ten toes, with her plain body with its particular scars, the story of a life made manifest?

So, as I begin my sure withering, I pluck the humble stories from my body, knowing that as I do I am not eminent or lofty or exceptional. I am but one of many, one of the hundreds, thousands, millions of bodies that have passed this way. I am one of the shabby crowd, nameless, singular.

Here's another thing: one day not long before she lost possession of her body, Nana Elsie told me that she could no longer find her lips. 'Someone's taken them,' she said, running manic fingers across her face.

I took her fingers and placed them on her lips. 'Look,' I said. 'Here they are.'

She ran her fingers across her lips, thin, feathered at the edges, lipstick-free (she, who always wore lipstick!). 'These aren't the ones,' she said.

I want to record the lips, the fingers, the belly, the tongue, before I forget they are mine.

FOUR

Sunshine

IN SPRING THE TRAPPED MOTHER put the baby in the pram in the garden. She parked the pram under a graceful purply-blue Sydney jacaranda, because she wanted a nutmeg-brown baby.

In this manner, the baby in the pram looked up to see a tenuous, flickering world. She saw the sky, the swaying trees, the blossoms rippling. The sun! Sunshine sparkled across her eyes and when she closed them, the sun was still visible, a tentacled light exploding outwards, a dance of warmth and brilliance, weightless.

This was the feeling of the loving sun on her newborn skin, as warm as a hand.

FIVE

My fingers

THE NIGHT I WAS BORN my mother cried. I was coated in fine dark hair and had a faint moustache and sideburns. My father's first remark when he saw me is recorded thus: 'I think she's the one who should be smoking the cigar.' The hair would soon fall out but my horrified mother did not know that. She was a famous beauty and I was not so much a disappointment as a disgrace.

While my mother was in labour my father was off screwing an old girlfriend. This is sad but true (just because something is a cliché does not mean—unfortunately—that it did not happen). When my father arrived at the hospital to make the crack about the cigar he had not bothered to shower. He leant over to kiss my mother and she smelt the unmistakeable scent of the female sex part.

She told me this story only once, when she was drunk. I do not know if she cried that night because of the ugliness of the baby, physical exhaustion following childbirth, or the unmistakeable scent of the female sex part.

·

My mother liked babies but she did not like the children they grew into. I was the eldest of three, with a younger brother and sister, and we recognised early that our mother did not want us. She was narcissistically self-absorbed, given to great howling speeches about how our father had wrecked her life.

Once, in winter, we came home from school to find the door locked. We could see our mother through the curtains, slumped in front of the television, drunk, dressed in a cocktail dress. She was wearing a turban.

Soon I found the comfort of my fingers. If a lover might be defined as one who loves, then I fell in love with my fingers, or perhaps my fingers fell in love with me.

My fingers are not beautiful. My hands are small like my mother's and even now that I am fully grown they are no larger than a child's. They have a certain fine-boned quality to them. My fingers are not long and elegant like a pianist's fingers but somewhat short with knobbly knuckles.

These same unlovely fingers led me to the rosy-tipped clitoris hidden in the folds of those other lips. Many times since I have witnessed the fat seeking fingers of baby girls, as unschooled as grubs, chance upon that rosy pulse.

The main incident you need to know about my childhood happened when I was nine. My mother had been drinking and my father had disappeared, as usual, to take a girl out for a drink or a fuck.

I surmise that when my mother finally heard my father's car tyres crunching over the newly laid red gravel of the driveway she raced into the kitchen and took the biggest knife she could find from the drawer. She then ran upstairs and dragged me from my dreaming bed to the top of the stairs so that when my father opened the front door he was confronted by the sight of my mother holding the tip of the knife against my throat.

'If you take another step I'll slit her throat,' she said.

'Ah . . . sweetheart,' my father replied. 'Listen . . .'

'Don't you sweetheart me,' said my mother.

My father tiptoed backwards out the door, leaving me at the mercy of the knife in my mother's trembling fingers. Fortunately for me, the moment my father closed the door my mother collapsed on the stairs, the knife falling.

When the knife was at my throat I left my body. That is to say, some part of me detached itself from my own skin. You might suppose that at the moment I left my body, I began my long quest to reunite myself with it.

SIX

Grass

SOON THE BABY MOVES FROM the pram to a blanket spread on the grass, and then rolls off the blanket and learns to stand upright.

The feel of grass beneath her feet is one of her earliest bodily memories. The baby does not weigh much and her feet are soft and unused, as silky and slippery as the ears of a freshly washed dog. The grass feels light beneath her feet, springy.

When the baby sits down, naked, because it is summer and the day is hot and she is not wearing a nappy, she feels for the first time the delicious half-ticklish, half-spiky feel of grass against her bottom, and smells the cut-open scent of it.

Grass smells like earth, like summer, like joy, and she tries to catch tiny blades of it in her fist, and to stuff it into her mouth. She longs to eat it, to have it inside herself, to *be* the grass, the blade, the smell of ripeness.

·

Once, grown, the woman is walking in a field near her house in Fanjeaux, France. It is a polished autumn morning and she notices that the tip of every single blade of grass holds a perfect dewdrop.

She gets down on her haunches to look more closely: everywhere she looks there are hundreds of shining, translucent orbs, spectral fruit, delicate, trembling.

She remembers too the feel of the wild, unnamed grasses she once lay on outside a stone house in the village of Soisy-sur-École, in the woods near Fontainebleau. It was early spring, and the winter had been harsh, and on this particular morning the sun came out with such violence she was shocked to discover that she had lived for so long behind the moon.

She did not walk out into the loving sun so much as rush into it and fall upon the grass in a swoon.

She lay on her back in a starfish shape, her wintery feet freed from shoes, her hands outstretched into the rhapsody of grass. Blades curled up between her fingers and weaved about her earlobes. It seemed to have grown overnight.

Turning her head her eyes were level with it so that the grass and the woman were as one, and she saw for the first time intricate white flowers, no bigger than her smallest fingernail, growing from the grass. She understood that the flowers, the racing grass, the root-world beneath, the whole of the natural world existed because of the nourishment of sunshine, falling leaves and water.

The world cracked open, in her eyes, in her ears, in her lungs: down on the ground, amid the sprouting grass and the earth's iceberg depths, she heard shackled nature growing, trying to revert to what it wanted to be.

SEVEN

The seventh lover

IT IS OFTEN TRUE THAT the prettiest of children grow into the plainest of adults, and the plainest of children emerge beautiful. In time I shed my freakish newborn hirsuteness, but kept a fine down on my arms and legs, in the manner of certain Greek or Turkish women. I have never needed to wax or bleach my moustache but now, occasionally, I pluck a stray wiry black hair from my chin. I take after my father. Sadly, I have never been beautiful.

What I am instead is what the French call *jolie laide*; that is, pretty and ugly, or unconventionally attractive. For a long time the thing that saved my face from obscurity was my mouth. It is my father's mouth, sensuous and plump, the upper lip full and well drawn. My front teeth are slightly prominent and once a lover, intending to compliment me, said my mouth frequently appeared enticingly open, ready, like a porn star's.

I grew into my adult face early. For years I looked older than I was, so that at sixteen I could pass for twenty, at twenty I could pass for twenty-six or twenty-seven. Fortuitously, sometime around my early thirties, I began to look younger than my age. This was a genetic fluke: after I lost my husband, when I was thirty-five, I took lovers ten years younger than myself and not one of them thought to ask how old I was.

Now the succulence of my pornographic mouth has left me. My lips, like my grandmother's, have left me. I am shameless about the violence of my physical ruin.

I have always had a well-developed musculature, an accident of birth, inherited from my mother. Before she took to drinking, my mother had been a swimming champion, at a national level, one of those doomed athletes who are good but not good enough. She did not make the team to represent her country at the 1956 Melbourne Olympic Games and so failed to reach international ranking.

I am no swimmer but I have my mother's aquatic limbs. At seven years of age my calves were honed like a diver's, and my thighs naturally sculpted. When I was dressed in a bathing costume or a pink ballet leotard, adults remarked that I had the physique of a gymnast. In ballet class, standing in front of the mirror practising my pliés at the barre, I first noticed the graceful scoop of my back and the plump rise of my buttocks.

Whenever anyone complimented me on the pleasing symmetry of my limbs I never thanked them. It seemed to me that this would be like expecting a thankyou from a tree, which had as much to do with the business of its appearance as I did. My mother did not take kindly to such compliments either, since the graceful ability of the body was exclusively her domain. 'You're all right, Deborah,' she said once, 'but you're nothing out of the box. I was exquisite when I was your age.'

The hairy girl has one other distinguishing feature. She first learns that it is a distinguishing feature the summer she turns seven, when she happens to walk naked past her mother who is lying in the bath, smoking.

'I don't remember my inner lips being so exposed when I was a girl,' her mother says.

'What?'

'Your inner lips. Normally the big outer lips cover the inner ones.'

The girl looks down at herself. 'What's wrong with them?'

The mother takes a drag of her cigarette and a long roll of ash drops into the water. 'Bugger,' she says, sitting up and placing the cigarette in the ashtray at the end of the bath. 'Perhaps they'll grow with the rest of you. I can't remember if they do or not.'

The girl is frightened she has done this to herself. Recently she has changed her masturbation technique: she has taken to lying on her stomach with her two index fingers on either side of what she has just learnt are her inner lips. Perhaps she has stretched them?

For years she believes she is the cause of her physical deformity.

·

That seven-year-old girl with the honed calves and the stretched inner lips, how did she know about desire? How did she find out that it spread up from that secret pulse, up and out through the inner lips and the outer, up through the fingers, the breath, and out into the world through the open mouth?

How did she come to be breathing so hot and so closely in a closed box with her brother?

Can it be true that the box had a lid, like a coffin? The girl thinks it does, a lid on two squeaky hinges, and when the lid is closed there is total darkness. There is nothing but the close breathing mouth of her brother, whose fingers are trying to find out the difference between a boy and a girl.

The first boy's fingers to touch that secret pulse are her brother's.

Have you ever noticed how many people marry someone who looks like their brother or sister, like a missing member of their family, no doubt unconsciously influenced by what is known as genetic sexual attraction?

Let that boy, my brother Paul, count as my seventh lover.

EIGHT

The first girl I loved

THE FIRST GIRL I LOVED had the whitest skin, as pale as an invalid's, and once, while playing leapfrog, she forgot to keep leaping but instead sat breathing with her legs spread upon my back.

I felt the pant of her breath on my neck, the race of her heart.

I felt the throb of her clitoris against the arch of my spine.

Neither of us moved.

I could have stayed like that for the rest of my life.

Nina Payne.

Nina Payne.

The whites of your eyes were white-blue like a newborn infant's.

Your upper gums showed when you smiled, glistening, moist.

I was jealous of your fringe. It rested against the high white dome of your forehead where I wished my lips could be.

·

Nina Payne's bedroom was at the back of her house. It was an old person's house, with old-fashioned, faded carpets and pink china figurines and a photograph of her father in a slouch hat and an army uniform. An only child, Nina Payne had elderly parents, at least as old as Nana Elsie.

We sometimes made cubbyhouses together. Mrs Payne let us take the good chairs from the dining room and blankets from the linen press into Nina Payne's girlish bedroom.

We holed ourselves up in our house in the dark and lay with our bodies pressed together, toe to toe.

We practised kissing, using our tongues, curling them deliciously around and around. Our tongues were entwined at their roots and once Nina Payne broke away, lifted up her long, swan-like neck and let out a moan.

I had never heard a sound like it before.

Immediately I wanted to hear it again.

The girl knew she was the boss of Nina Payne. Nina Payne was docile, practically mute, and the girl with the strange inner lips was the one who directed the play. She arranged when they would meet, at what time and at which house. The girl made her friend pretend to be a nurse while she lay in the dark of the cubbyhouse and made Nina Payne run her fingers over her body inch by inch to check for disease.

She made Nina Payne take off her underpants and walk around the yard in her dress, while the girl lay on the ground and looked up. She made Nina Payne sit with her legs apart so that she could see for herself whether she had a distinguishing feature like hers.

Nina Payne's vagina was pale, only slightly rosier than the rest of her.

The girl would have stuck her finger in except that her friend stood up and ran away.

In lying down with Nina Payne, in sucking her tongue and her strange, supine lips, the girl may indeed have been seeking the maternal body.

There was so much space between her mother and herself.

NINE

Object-sexualist

PERHAPS YOU HAVE HEARD OF the Swedish woman who took as her lover the Berlin Wall. Eija-Ritta Berliner-Mauer, known as Mrs Berlin Wall since she married her lover on 17 June 1979, describes herself as an object-sexualist. By this Mrs Berlin Wall means that she is emotionally and sexually attracted to objects, and believes them to have souls, feelings and desires. As an animist, she thinks all objects are living: 'If one can see objects as living things, it is also pretty close to be able to fall in love with them.'

Eija-Ritta Berliner-Mauer lives quietly in a village in Sweden, surrounded by objects she has fallen in love with. The central figure in her life remains her now-broken husband.

Many people speak of loving houses—a particular house in which they were happy, or one in which they spent their wondrous first years. Some people speak of loving gardens, the contours of which are as familiar as a beloved face.

I once loved the jasmine that covered the side of the house in Sydney where I grew up, which every spring burst into starry blossom.

Brick.

Wall.

House.

The lover as object.

It is a private matter between the object lover and ourselves to know if the object lover loves us back.

I have not seen *Berlinmuren*, the film about Eija-Ritta Berliner-Mauer by the Norwegian artist Lars Laumann. I do not speak Swedish or Norwegian and my German is basic so the only words in the German reviews of the film I could make out were: 'sex with the Berlin Wall'. When I close my eyes I see a thin, greying woman with her arms outspread, capturing nothing. Perhaps she engages in the gentle art of frotting any surviving bricks she owns, or maybe she mounts them.

In my mind's eye, the house in which Mrs Berlin Wall dwells looks like a cottage in a fairytale, deep in a dark Swedish forest. It has smoke coming from a chimney and I see her at the window, sitting at a long blond-wood table, the surface of which is adorned with bricks and barbed wire. Throughout the house are framed photographs of her retired husband in his vigorous prime.

In the bedroom, on the sheets and on the pillow, is a scattering of clay, dark, ruddy, smeared like blood. It is here, in the night, that Eija-Ritta communes most deeply with the object of her affections. In granting life to an inanimate object I imagine she is the very epitome of an intellectual; that is, giving breath to an idea—in this case to some sublime idea of division, of partition, of *wallness*. It seems to me that Mrs Berlin Wall's devotion is an act more of mental life than of bodily life, but then again I am not there when her open mouth turns to the smear of dark clay beside her on the pillow and her love is suddenly made flesh.

It is true that I, too, have taken objects as my lovers: a car, a garden, a house. Longing for a house once entered my bloodstream like lust and for seven summers I rushed to this house, my heart wild in my chest, and I could hardly wait for my feet to touch its cool white tiles.

TEN, ELEVEN, TWELVE

Cheese—Chocolate—Croissants

UNLIKE MRS BERLIN WALL, HOWEVER, I could never marry an object that did not pulse with blood, or did not require light or rain in order to live. I might have an affair with a house, but I could never marry one. I could never marry anything without a mouth.

My mouth is the opening into myself, the principal portal of the body: the teeth, the gums, the fleshy slope of the throat, the glistening entrance into the dark depths below. The myriad tastebuds of the tongue which, when I was young, I imagined resembled the buds on the frangipani tree outside our house.

I pictured a tongueful of flowers, smaller than the eye could see, hundreds of tender buds opening as one to savour the body's bountiful catch.

.

From my earliest days I have had affairs with the food that gives my body life. Food may be mouthless but it is nonetheless animate, created by the dance of water, heat and light.

I have had endless affairs with fat French cheeses, creamy and sticky, made from raw cow's milk, brought to full, ripe life through the confluence of time and air. The rich distinctive smell of a mature brie de Melun has spilt into my nose and mouth, causing my mouth to flood with water and desire.

I have been a lover of milky chocolate dissolving on my tongue, of the dreamy bloom of thick, sensuous fragrance that spreads up from the tongue to the roof of the mouth, to light up all the pleasure receptors of the brain.

And then there is the croissant. Such a brief, perishing object! So full of life, yet as evanescent as the most fragile butterfly, dead by day's end, its flowering over within hours. *Le feuilletage*, layer upon layer of pastry animated by yeast, alive with butter, rolled and folded as carefully as an old-fashioned handwritten letter.

In the northern hemisphere croissants have a season, like asparagus or cherries, and the croissant's season is brief, from the end of October to the beginning of November. After this, the wheat harvests of summer are blended with older harvests, and the pastry made from blended wheat becomes inferior.

The particular warm, satisfying fragrance of a proper croissant *au beurre* in season, preferably eaten at a café in Paris on a pale autumn day, fresh out of the oven, warm and alive.

The whiff of the egg wash in the moment before the croissant enters the mouth and is felt upon the tongue. The crisp golden flakes surrounding its moist heart, flakes as sharp as toast, which crackle as you bite into it. Pierre Hermé, the renowned Parisian *pâtissier*, says that the sign of a good croissant is that you should be able to hear its suffering as you eat it.

The tongue is the last to forget desire: my mother's tongue loved chocolate, avocado and cream right up until the end, when at last her tongue of flowers forgot the sound of suffering.

THIRTEEN

The smell of love

MY FATHER CAME FROM A long line of braggarts and fools, mainly dirt-poor Scots given to making a great deal of money before losing it.

In general we might be called history's bit players. In his youth my foolish great-great-grandfather once shared a cell with the iconic Australian bushranger Ned Kelly. My great-great-grandfather was in jail for debt, in Beechworth prison to be precise, and the only helpful thing he recorded in his diaries about Ned Kelly was that he snored manfully.

This same relative, who, even in his dotage, was given to taking off for newly discovered goldfields at the drop of a hat, once met the author Mark Twain in 1895 while travelling on a ship from San Francisco to Sydney. Apparently Mark Twain, who introduced himself as Sam, confided to my great-great-grandfather his belief that dreaming was better than reality. The journal in which my forebear noted this comment has now been lost but I remember reading this journal in my twenties and being struck by how my relative kept missing the point. For example, on the day he married Mademoiselle Emilie Joubert—the daughter of a baker from Angers and believed to be descended from Huguenots—he failed to mention his marriage at all, noting instead the specifics of the weather.

Perhaps it is my splash of French blood, bequeathed to me by the long-dead Mademoiselle Emilie Joubert, which leads me to the adoration of the croissant. But perhaps poor Mademoiselle Emilie Joubert preferred a crusty *tartine* over a croissant? A baguette fresh from the oven, split in two, spread thickly with butter and jam made from red berries, dipped in a bowl of warm coffee.

Perhaps when she found herself living in a tent next to a stream in the middle of Victoria, Australia, because her new husband believed there was gold in it, she dreamed of *tartines*. In the early, bird-filled mornings she might have woken to find the smell of them in her nostrils, so rich, so true, that it hurt to realise her own memory had been baking them. There was no oven, no father standing next to it, no fine, flowery Viron flour turned by heat into the smell of love.

Where are Mademoiselle Joubert's phantom *tartines* now? Where are her body's memories, her cherished recall of freshly baked baguettes which smelt like love?

Mademoiselle Joubert's husband never wrote down her memories. In his journals he noted the sky, the gold, the manful snores of Ned Kelly, but all Mademoiselle Joubert's bodily store—her recall of flour, with its residue of ash which left a fine powder on her fingertips, of the sharp, singing taste on her tongue of *fleur de sel de Guérande*, the champagne of salt, and especially the smell of bread and love in the morning—have disappeared.

I once loved the fragrance of leather in the handbag shop where Nana Elsie spent her working life.

I absorbed into myself the rich scent of cured animal hide, redolent of distant grasses, plains and valleys. Leather smelt of love in that dark cave of a shop of fine Italian leather goods in every shade of cream, brown and black, that cave of shiny gold buckles and folds of softest suede.

FOURTEEN

Mother's red fingernails

MY MOTHER WAS A PRACTISED back scratcher. She kept her nails long and one of the great thrills of my life was discovering that the nail file she used to keep the edges of each nail rounded and smooth was made of diamonds. The earth's most precious stone, pressed into service so that my mother might keep her fingernails tidy.

She let me inspect the nail file, shot through with brilliance, with glittering flecks that flashed like stars. The file finished in a cruel tip, curled like a hook, which could easily scoop out an eye.

I would sometimes lie face down beside my mother on the bed or the sofa and pull up my top in a wordless signal to her that I wanted my back scratched. More often than not she would bat me away, too engrossed in whatever book she was reading. She was a great reader, anything from *Peyton Place* and *Gone with the Wind* to *Love in a Cold Climate*. She was particularly fond of Dickens. But sometimes she would smile down at me in a preoccupied, absent-minded way and reach out to run her long, red-painted nails lightly over the skin of my back. Her fingernails drew intoxicating patterns, arabesques and whirls, inducing wafts of sensory pleasure that stupefied me. Sometimes they passed across the surface of my skin in loose, feathery circles, and sometimes they traced a firmer line that followed some secret path only my mother knew. Occasionally her fingernails moved too close to the small of my back, to the place that tickled, and then my whole body arched in an ecstatic involuntary shiver.

FIFTEEN

Giggling

SHE IS NOT SUPPOSED TO remember the night that her sister was born but her body remembers her father gathering them up, the girl and her brother, and a long, flickering, dreamlike drive through deserted Sydney streets.

In the week her sister Jane was born the local creek flooded and her mother and the new baby could not come home because the carpet was wet. The girl remembers feeling cold on the way to the hospital, a new unpleasant feeling she could not name twisting up her guts, for the body is always first to get the news.

She was a beauty, was Jane. My mother, June, came from a long line of beauties. Milky Irish beauties for the most part, rosy-lipped and white of skin and teeth. June was one, and her mother Elsie too. Nana Elsie was so beautiful as a small child that one day as she was playing in the garden of the house where she lived in Orange, New South Wales, a rich childless couple stopped and begged to adopt her. And in her youth Nana Elsie's mother Lil, my great-grandmother, was famous for being the most beautiful girl in Orange. Lil was the daughter of Joseph, an Irishman who owned the finest hotel in town. We called her Super Nan to distinguish her from Nana Elsie.

Jane belonged: pale, translucent skin, blue eyes, grey at the centre, like a Siamese cat's. Grown, her face carried the secret blueprint of beauty, in that its symmetry matched that composite face used in tests by advertisers and market researchers and university students to find out which particular human face is considered the loveliest. Jane's face was mathematically correct: oval, with the right symmetry between forehead, eyebrow and cheekbone, between mouth and jaw.

The girl's body knew something was up. She stood shivering in the rain, looking up at the hospital room where her mother and the new baby were sleeping. 'Look, up there!' said her father. 'Mummy's up there. Wave!'

It was night. It was raining. The hospital was closed to visitors and, anyway, in those days hospitals did not let children visit new babies because of germs.

They stood shivering in the rain, waving at the darkened building, at the mother they could not see, at an invisible baby with a beautiful face somewhere inside. June and Jane, mother and daughter, so alike even their names were distinguished by only a single letter: June, Jane, tick and tock, the beginning and the end.

When Jane grew up she had golden curls, like a girl in a story. She wore them in two pretty plaits and when the girl was eight she cut off one of her sister's golden plaits: snip.

She should have been ashamed of herself.

She was old enough to know better.

She was, perhaps, prefiguring the future. You might say that, in a modest way, she was avenging her coming self.

The sister grew up to possess the most magnificent giggle you have ever heard, the kind you wanted to cause for the pleasure of hearing it.

Jane's giggle was like a rinse of sun, an unexpected present, and had the effect of making you happy. Getting Jane down on the bed and seeing her collapse her beautiful neck in order to escape the fingers trying to reach her most tickly spot was a joy beyond words. The hot pant of her breath, the flushed face, the giggling in her which set up an answering giggle in you so that before long all your insides were shaken up, exultant, and there was nothing but the happiness of flopping back exhausted on the bed, the giggling having pumped everything noxious from you and rinsed you clean. You should have known that one day you would wish to cut the giggle from her throat.

SIXTEEN

The dog who loved me

NOT JUST ANY DOG, a prince among dogs. A chocolate labrador, a silky short-haired gun dog with a chocolate-coloured nose to match his coat, name of Rhett.

At first an unruly puppy, lurking under tables, nipping childish toes. Little pointed shark-like teeth, razor sharp, soon to fall out, and the more you squealed, the more he believed your toes and legs to be a moveable entertainment designed especially for him. Loose in his skin, a soft, downy armful, a face sweeter than a baby's, but soon a digger of holes to China, kidnapper of socks, chewer of shoes. Named by my mother for Rhett Butler from *Gone with the Wind*—the bookish Rhett and not the Hollywood actor, Clark Gable.

'What's the difference?' I asked when I was sixteen, and Rhett was on his last legs.

'In my mind Rhett Butler in the book doesn't look a thing like Clark Gable,' my mother said.

'Does he look like a chocolate labrador?' I asked.

She gave me a withering look. 'You are a very literal-minded girl, Deborah,' she said. 'You have no imagination.'

This was one of her favourite put-downs. She said it about my deflowerer, Jonathan Jamieson, he of the wounded, dark-lashed brown eyes and the caramel-coloured skin, the singer of songs, the first boy who loved me.

The dog had a straight, powerful tail, thick at the base and slightly tapered at the end so that when wet (he loved to swim) it resembled the tail of an otter. Wet, the whole of Rhett resembled an otter or a seal, the plump meat of his dark back and stomach glisteningly revealed. There was something liquid about him in general, too, in the swift, effortless way he moved in space, in his remarkably moist chestnut-coloured eyes, full of sympathy and helpless love. He readily proffered the wet snout of friendship, and he had a knack for endless fluid patience, for standing still for hours while frilly bonnets were wrapped around his head and skirts draped across his back.

A vocal dog, given to loud theatrical yawns, and groans of erotic pleasure when stroked. Neither before nor since have I come across a dog who so clearly signalled his joy: when I held Rhett against the length of my body, when I was still so small that the span of a warm outstretched dog from tail to snout was greater than my own, he emitted long, satisfied groans in my ear. I felt his heartbeat, lighter and faster than a human's, as if all his life was being used up more quickly. I lay with him in my arms on the carpet or on the grass, and he gave out great, hot sighs.

.

My father owned a travel agency, which meant our family got cheap
international airfares. This was in the early days of jets, when
flying was thrilling and strange, an exclusive privilege granted
to the rich and the exotic, and we were frequent flyers before the
term was invented. (Travel, too, gave my father the chance to fly
in and out of our lives like a man on a magic carpet.) When we
flew away, to Disneyland or Fiji or New York, Rhett moved to a
kennel. It was always the same kennel, Waggin' Tails, and somehow
Rhett always knew the moment he was put in the car that he was
being packed off. All the way to Waggin' Tails he howled, a head-
thrown-back, deep-throated whine of misery. We tried everything:
furtively packing his water and food bowls in the car in the dead
of the night before, investigating new and more labyrinthine ways
of negotiating the streets to the kennel door. How did he know we
weren't going to the beach or to the national park for a picnic?
How did he know he was on his way to incarceration at Waggin'
Tails and the enforced friendships of other dogs, to long, sad days
of separation from everyone he loved?

At the kennel car park we had to wrestle him out of the car.
My brother Paul and I attempted to take one end and my father
the other but it always ended in a wild scramble of nails, hair
and teeth and my father picking up Rhett and carrying him in.
When Rhett was set on the floor of Waggin' Tails' reception area,
his last-ditch attempt was to put on the brakes, to concentrate
the full force of his muscular twenty-five-kilo body into his stiff,

unmoving legs. We had to drag him down the corridor, his four legs comically extended like a dog in a cartoon, his nails skidding on the linoleum. It was like pulling a small truck or a dead body, but when we finally wrestled him into a cage all the weight went out of him, and all his puff. He accepted defeat, floating to the floor as if he suddenly weighed no more than a kitten.

Rhett comforted me when I was sad, resting his large, understanding head against mine while I cried. I do not think it is anthropomorphic projection to say that Rhett felt unhappy when I was unhappy, and happy when I was happy, and that we shared some magical, speechless accord. He had a keen empathy, the ability to swiftly assess emotional temperature and to align himself with it. Rhett had his own strong, independent emotions, too; he could get jealous, for example, and when I patted other dogs he instinctively batted them away, giving them a sharp nip around the ears for good measure.

If I have ever had another lover who loved me more, his name is a secret.

SEVENTEEN

Flight

ON FIRST SEEING THE CLOUDS below me, those great swelling blooms of vapour, those mountains of air, I was confirmed in my love of going somewhere. The earth was free and the sky was open! I was suspended in time, or rather travelling in it, my body and time as one, moving through space, through matter, through the wonders of enigmatic existence.

Movement enraptured me, or, more particularly, *sic gloria transit mundi*, a sudden apprehension of the passing glories of the world. In flight I was a body transported, joined to all that passing glory, and it did not matter where I was from, or where I was going.

EIGHTEEN

The perfect lover

WHEN I TURNED TEN, A fizz of adrenaline lit up my veins, causing my breath to come fast, making me bounce from foot to foot as if in preparation for a race.

Every afternoon I experienced a queasy mixture of excitement, shyness and anticipation as I waited with sweating palms, a thumping heart and a dry, hot mouth for *The Monkees* television show.

I was at the beginning of my desire to dash myself against the perfect lover, perpetually out of range, in the form of a boy or man who would never love me back. The Monkees drummer, Micky Dolenz, was my first lover in that dream in which no matter how hard we dream, the perfect lover remains beyond.

Later, even when certain lovers breathed into my face, they were still afar.

NINETEEN

Cigarettes

I AM NO LONGER SUPPOSED to smoke. I am supposed to recognise the cigarette for the lethal drug it is, for its toxic mix of chemicals and death. But certain men and women are known for falling towards what is wounding with what can only be described as open-hearted intent. For someone like me, raised by a spoilt man wreathed in smoke, weaned by a red-nailed, ash-covered beauty, the cigarette has a seductive, hypnotic pull.

I love the cigarette's siren call to my mouth, the rude intimacy of holding a cigarette between my lips. I love the sensuous connection between the round filtered tip of a cigarette and the nipple, the suck of it, the drawing in. I love a cigarette's poisonous spill into my blood, the electric rush of nicotine to my brain. Because I don't smoke often, the first cigarette hits my nerves and blood and heart in one hot druggy rush, a venomous blossoming in my lungs that sometimes makes me lean against the nearest thing for fear that I might faint.

TWENTY

Her father

A GIRL WHO HAS FELT the knife against her throat and imagined that upon her tongue blooms a thousand flowers naturally falls in love with her father.

The girl's father is a charismatic and glamorous figure to her, and she quickly takes his side over her mother's. She is perhaps obeying some deep unconscious impulse to win the father from the mother, since the mother is her rival for his love. It is not uncommon for a girl to try out her emerging sexuality on her father, but when that father is a man compulsively driven to seduce as many women as possible, this may prove a fatal introduction.

Her father never tries to seduce the girl in a literal sense, but he seduces her into a world of sexually incontinent, feckless men, so that for many years the only men she finds attractive will betray her.

•

The afternoon Sharon from the office calls her father at home the girl instinctively knows to lie when her mother asks who is on the phone. 'It's Nina,' she says.

'Haven't you just said goodbye to her?' her mother remarks. 'I don't know what you girls find to talk about.'

It is true that the girl speaks to Nina Payne at recess and at lunchtime and then talks to her all the way home. She speaks to her on the telephone every afternoon, too. But the days have long passed since Nina Payne was the girl's sexual slave and they never talk about that time. They never talk either about whether Nina Payne is better-looking than the girl, or whether the girl is better-looking than Nina Payne, although this is the true subject that concerns them. They are squaring up to their futures, trying to find out what each girl carries in her basket.

When her father gets home, the girl waits until her mother has left the room before she tells him Sharon called. He is mixing himself a martini, his new favourite drink, and before him on the coffee table are some brochures for the new hotel he is going to take them to in New York.

'What did she want?' her father asks.

'Guess,' she replies.

Her father looks up from the business of ice cubes and silver tongs (it is the days of cocktail shakers and ice-cube holders). It seems to her that he looks at her properly for the first time in her life. She feels dazzled, singled out, special. She is twelve years old.

He sips his drink and lights another cigarette.

Then he smiles.

Soon after this the girl happens to catch sight of her father and Sharon sitting together in a parked car not far from the travel agency. She is walking Rhett, who is taking his time investigating the bouquet of urine left against a fence by some previous dog. While waiting for Rhett to finish his sniffing, the girl chances to look into the car containing her father and his girlfriend.

Sharon is crying and her father ineffectually tries to make her stop. He leans across from the driver's seat to stroke her golden hair (straight from the bottle) and in doing so sees the girl. He nods at her before gesturing that she should move on: *Nick off*, this gesture says.

The girl yanks the lead. 'Come on, Rhett. Come on, boy.'

It is not until three days later, when her father is driving the girl to Nina's house, that they speak about what she saw.

'About the other day,' her father says. 'Don't jump to conclusions.'

She doesn't say anything.

'You don't know anything about the complications of life,' he says.

The girl looks out the window. For some time she has been practising keeping her expression as impassive as possible, so that not a single trace of anything she keeps inside can be found upon her face. After a while she leans over and switches on the radio.

'Life's more mysterious than you could possibly imagine, Debs,' her father says. 'Remember that.'

She has not forgotten.

I slept with the man who slept with the girl who slept with
the man who slept with the girl who slept with Bob Dylan

Does this mean Bob and I are connected?

A lover's kiss

A KISS CAN BE POTENT.

In the legend of the frog prince, the prince's kiss represents the discovery of selfhood. The kiss symbolises the transition to maturity, a maiden's readiness for marriage.

Once, in London on New Year's Eve, traffic prevented me from being at the party where I was supposed to be. At midnight I found myself alone in the back of a black cab, caught in a traffic jam.

We were stuck in Westminster, right beside Big Ben, when I heard the bells start up. Suddenly I wanted to hear them with my unwrapped ears, to hear time being counted out as we passed through it. I leant over and tapped on the screen separating me from the taxi driver.

'Can you wind the window down, please, so I can hear the bells?'

'It's bloody freezing,' he said, but lowered the windows so the thrilling air rushed in, bearing with it the complicated, pealing sound of time passing.

I turned my face up to the icy air, to the bells, to the gold of the clock tower lit up against the black winter night, and as midnight struck a beautiful stranger leant into the taxi and kissed me.

TWENTY-THREE

The beery-mouthed lover

EVERY SUMMER THE GIRL AND her family travelled north from Sydney to visit the father's widowed mother, Dorothy, a stiff-backed Methodist who had turned out two boys, one as stiff-backed as herself, the other their spoilt, ruined father. The father was the younger son, in love with his mother, who could not resist her youngest son's charms.

As they drove north the air grew damp with heat, sweet with the smell of vegetable decay. They drove with the windows down, on roads that were not yet proper highways, and outside were strangler figs and mango trees and mosquitoes and the peppery scent of lantana. They drove for two days and a night, and in that night the cane fields on either side burnt, flames against the black, birds and snakes and rats flying and shrieking as they fled the crackling hell.

When they stopped to cross dark rivers on flat-bottomed barges, the girl and her brother and sister were allowed out into the tropical air. Their mother remained slumped in the front seat of the hot, dispirited car, a damp cloth across her forehead.

'Queensland gives me a headache,' she said.

The father sighed.

'Why am I always surrounded by people sighing?' the mother said.

Standing by the railing, watching the black river twisting as they passed over it, the world turned mysterious and scented, the sky strung with stars which seemed closer to heaven, and every now and then bats swung in fantastic triangular patterns across the darkness. The sky was black beyond blackness, depthless, immense, embracing more than the naked eye could measure.

In this entwined, strangled place the girl's body bled for the first time. She awoke one morning in her grandmother's starched-sheeted bed to feel wetness between her legs. Her fingers came up sticky, red, and in bringing her fingers into the light she stained the white sheets with streaks of virginal blood. When she stood up, she saw blood on the white sheet.

She tried to wash the sheets in the bathroom but the blood spilt out into a pink, flooding stain and she stood in a river of blood, tears and water until her mother knocked on the door to ask what was going on.

Her mother gave her a little cloth purse with two Modess sanitary napkins inside, first demonstrating how to hook the pad to the elastic belt.

'When I was a girl we didn't have pads and belts,' she said. 'We used plain old washers. We had to rinse them out.' A tenderness flickered across her face. 'You're a woman now,' she said. 'Poor thing. Don't worry about the mattress, it'll dry in the sun.'

Coming out of the bathroom, they came across the father. 'Deb's little eggs have come down,' the mother announced.

All day the drying mattress with its interlocked rings of stains rested against the steps of the back veranda.

In this entwined, strangled place they went to stay at a beach house belonging to friends of the parents. The friends were television journalists, the father a famous face from the nightly news. The girl could hardly raise her eyes to look at him.

The journalists had two teenage daughters, older than the girl, nubile, bursting out of their tawny skins, with heavy eye make-up and Hawaiian-print bikinis tied at their hips. The older daughter had a deep, heavy bosom and looked like a grown woman. She immediately asked if she could do the girl's make-up.

Afterwards, she insisted on parading the girl in front of the drunken adults, who were having a party on the deck overlooking the beach. When the girls joined them a cheer went up, wolf whistles, claps.

'She's hot to trot,' said the man with the famous face. 'What's the bet she's a real goer?'

'Just like her dad,' said the wife of the man with the famous face, kissing the girl's father full on his sensuous lips.

The father did not smile but looked at the girl with a strange expression.

'She looks like a slut,' said the mother.

The girl looked down in an agony of embarrassment, trying to hide herself. She was wearing a Modess sanitary pad and was already anxious about how she was going to dispose of it. She believed everybody could see the pad beneath her clothes.

Her bones were too big for her, her legs ungainly, her arms as skinny as gnawed chicken bones. The finely honed calves and thighs once taken for those of a gymnast were no longer. She did not fit her own skin, as if overnight she had outgrown her child self but had not yet formed into someone new. But atop her awkward body was a face that eyeliner, false eyelashes, blusher and lipstick had transformed.

In this entwined, strangled place, boys came. Boyfriends of the tawny, bosomy girls, and other boys. On the beach at night, with the sound of the waves and faraway noiseless heaven, a fire was lit in the sand and couples paired off to lie on towels and blankets.

The girl shivered, afraid, alone, even though the night was peopled; the air dense with a thick moist heat which clung to her skin. She wanted to go inside to be with the other children. She had defied her mother and was still wearing make-up, except now the make-up felt like a mask, under which she was a frightened imposter. A slow, sluggish horror was growing in her, an animal fear, and the girl no longer wished to be a teenager. One of the boys, an older boy of seventeen or eighteen, came over and sat down next to her on the towel, passing her his bottle of beer. She took a swig and it hit the back of her throat, gaseous, sour.

'I like you,' the boy said, his voice swollen with emotion. Even as he finished speaking his beery mouth came towards her, resting slimily against her own. At the same time he pulled her hand down to the great boned thing in his trousers. His other hand dived painfully between her legs and he shouted, 'Hey! She's on the rag!' The girl sprang up and ran back towards the house, her lungs bursting, all the while believing she was being chased like a runaway horse, was about to be brought down.

She was crying by the time she reached her brother and sister, who were inside watching television, eating Twisties and drinking Coca-Cola with the smaller children. Everyone looked up as she rushed in, gulping, tears ruining the beautiful mask. She ran past them to the bathroom where she slammed the door, locking it behind her.

She wanted to stay locked inside for the rest of her life, beyond the reach of the nameless thing outside.

TWENTY-FOUR

A horse

LET ME NOT FORGET THE autumn of the horse. That autumn when I begged and begged my mother to let me go riding, after falling in love with sitting with my legs spread wide, not wearing jodhpurs like the other girls but a pair of thin pants, the hard leather of the saddle and the motion of the warm horse between my legs, moving in the open air, unpeeling, while sitting up and passing through the trees.

TWENTY-FIVE

The first lover who entered my body

WHEN NANA ELSIE WAS A girl, just before motherhood claimed her, she kissed a boy in Orange. Orange is a fruit-growing district, rich in apples, pears and stone fruit such as cherries, peaches, apricots and plums. A high-up place where it sometimes snows in winter, Orange has the wrong climate for oranges.

Nana Elsie kissed the boy at the railway station, just before the train arrived to take him away. For a long while afterwards, she used to walk to the station and look with longing down the tracks.

Like Nana Elsie, I sometimes look back with longing. I think of the first lover who entered my body, how gently he held me, and how my life had left me unprepared for such a kind and steady hold.

TWENTY-SIX

The knee-trembler

THE FIRST TIME A STRANGER reached into the girl's underpants and found the sliver of flesh at the centre of her, her knees folded in surprise.

At the time the girl was in Sydney, Australia, about to walk as many miles as she could for the flooded children of Bangladesh. Men were on the moon but certain citizens of North Vietnam were living in tunnels beneath the earth.

The girl was not yet walking though; she was standing up, pressed against a wall which formed part of St Ives High School, in what she would later learn was the classic knee-trembler position. Her dress was bunched up around her bum, her mouth was open, and if the boy whom she hardly knew had not held her up she might have fallen.

He was a big boy for fifteen, tall, with wide shoulders, and a dark rinse of hair across his upper lip which he would soon start to shave. He was offhand, cruel, not kind and steady, and he held her in a way she would come to know well, but which she felt for the first time in that moment: a larger body than her own encircling hers, engulfing her, yet at the same time empowering her. The way the boy stood over her, claiming her, placing one hand tight against her lower back, the other hand in her pants, running his fingers in light, feathery strokes over that sliver of flesh with its secret pulse, his tongue deep in her mouth, well, she suddenly understood the full nature of her femaleness.

She felt herself being unlocked.

She felt herself to be embodied, to be experiencing herself as a material thing, as a heart, a spine, a stomach, a womb, yet in the same second she knew herself to be dispossessed.

She was a daydream, a breath, nothing other than what the body wanted.

TWENTY-SEVEN

Nana Elsie

TICK-TOCK. TICK-TOCK. WHAT else does the body know? What else does the breathing heart remember?

Like a daguerreotype, that beautiful, abandoned photographic process through which an image is produced on a thin copper plate with a highly polished silver coating, the past floats up, water-damaged, faded, obscured by curious markings.

A cloudy vapour shrouds an event here, a remark there, and brown and black rings blot out entire faces. In the 1850s, daguerreotypes were kept sealed beneath a piece of glass, and in the house of the stiff-backed Methodist grandmother there was a stained photograph of Mademoiselle Emilie Joubert, newly arrived in Australia, but the glass was gone. Most often it is not just the glass seal which has gone from our memories, but the images beneath them.

.

The body remembers. The body remembers happiness in a warm childhood bed, with her mother, her brother, her sister and the grandmother she loved best of all.

Sometimes Nana Elsie stayed for the weekend. After the father got up, the children and the grandmother joined the mother in the marital bed. The girl's mother cuddled her mother like a child, and everyone cuddled the person they were next to, a huddle of bodies, ankle against ankle, a fug of human breath. They cuddled like this for many years until one day the brother said he didn't want to cuddle anymore.

In that bed, Nana Elsie told them stories. She told them about the time she put a doll's eye up her nose and how the doctor got it out with a pair of especially long tweezers. She told them about her mother, Super Nan, whose husband had proved to be the jealous type. When he came back from the Great War to find yet another child (Super Nan had not known she was pregnant when he left) he refused to acknowledge paternity and kept her under lock and key. He burnt all her clothes and cut off her hair and she was only ever allowed out if accompanied by him or one of her eleven children. She finally escaped when her youngest child was five, and her husband went around looking for them with a gun. 'Dad was a big fellow, too,' Nana Elsie said.

Nana Elsie had a radiance about her person. The whites of her eyes were whiter than any the girl had ever seen. They were those luminous blue eyes you rarely see, deep-set, the kind that made you think they were *true* eyes, and that all other eyes were faulty copies of the real thing.

The girl had to hide her love for Nana Elsie from her mother. She had to pretend it was less ardent than it was.

'You've got a thing for your grandmother,' the mother said. 'You only like her because she thinks everyone's wonderful. She's got her head in the sand.'

The girl wanted her head in the sand too. She wanted shared sand to fill her ears, her nose, her throat, to be swamped by the same lucky sand as Nana Elsie.

TWENTY-EIGHT

The music lover

THE GIRL DISCOVERED HER EARS, the sounds that poured into them, breathing and waves and birds and cicadas and shouting and criticism and admonishments and coos but, best of all, music. Music! How she loved it, its mysterious ability to alter mood, to slice the heart, a shimmering door to rapture. The Monkees were gone, but after them came The Beatles' *Abbey Road*, Neil Young's *Harvest* and Carole King's *Tapestry* played over and over. Music entered the bloodstream, more pure than any drug, intense, luminous. Music entered the air, dancing invisibly upon it before vanishing to some unreachable place, gone like the wind and the dead.

Once, not long after she met the lover she was going to marry, the lover she loved so much she feared she might die of astonished joy, the woman travelled in a car. She was sitting in the back of a rented car, driving from Paris to Normandy for the weekend. As the car slid along the road at dusk the Normandy sky of the painters rose up, a rinse of pink and grey and gold, the net of heaven. It was hot, the windows were open, and Miles Davis's 'So What' was playing. The hypnotising pulse of the music mirrored the metronomic beat of her pulse, the pump of her heart, everything in her that was set like a clock, everything rhythmic and moving and alive. The music soared through her, in her hair, in the coils of her ears, under her nails. Forever after, whenever she hears 'So What', she is young, free and soaring.

TWENTY-NINE

A cat

AS WELL AS A DOG I also had a cat called Miss Meow. She was black and white, with large green eyes and a pearly pink nose, luscious, like a pink marshmallow. She resembled a pretty young girl, lipsticked and mascaraed. Miss Meow was elegant and fussy, and looked like she should be wearing a pair of fine shoes and a tiara.

Sometimes she would lick my arms with her thin, scratchy tongue. Her tongue had raised pink points on it but if you looked closely enough you could see they were actually bristles, like the neat row of bristles on a cheap plastic hairbrush. It is very hard to catch a cat's tongue between your fingers.

Miss Meow's tongue made a scraping sound against the fur of my arms. She licked thoroughly, judiciously. She licked me from my fingers to the inside of my forearm right up to my shoulder while I tried not to move, lying as still as I could bear.

THIRTY

Jonathan Jamieson

THE GIRL TRAVELLED THE GLOBE with her chaotic parents at a time when jet travel was exotic, and most people could only dream about it.

It seemed beyond the realms of possibility that she should travel so far. Sometimes, waking up in a hotel room and stealing out of bed to look out the window before anyone else was awake, the girl felt unspeakably happy because she was in an unknown place.

Such a girl might start to dream of weaving her own rug on which to fly away. Such a girl might not yet know that it is not only in fables that running away leads inevitably back to the source of our dread.

For now, all the girl knows is that she feels safer walking away from the house with the mother and father, the sister and brother, the cat and the dog, than walking towards it. She does not like to bring friends home in case her mother is drunk and wearing a turban, or else not drunk but plunged into one of her moods, sarcastic, bitter, watchful.

'You're not very clever, are you?' she said to the girl one after-noon, as her brother Paul tried to teach the girl how to play poker, which she could not fathom, especially knowing that her mother was watching.

The mother, June, was not able to control herself like other people. She could not hold her tongue, keep the peace or under-stand that discretion was the better part of valour. Whatever she felt spilt out from her, whole, without pause or refinement. Her emotions were cartoonishly big, without fences or boundaries.

The day arrived when the girl brought her lover home. She was sixteen, about to turn seventeen, in love with her deflowerer, Jonathan Jamieson, he of the wounded, dark-lashed brown eyes and the caramel-coloured skin, the singer of songs, the first boy who loved her. He was kind and steady, and held her gently, and for as long as she was able the girl resisted bringing Jonathan Jamieson home, being fearful of the turban, the father on his magic carpet, the sister who was more beautiful than her.

But fear should evoke our gratitude for its ability to reveal us to ourselves. Fear reveals the things we love, and without it to tell us what it is we find most precious, we might never know what we love at all.

.

Over the years the mother had devised a series of cunning etiquette tests. It is not true that Australia is classless, and the mother enjoyed nothing better than setting tabletop traps. She would lay out soup spoons and dessert spoons and fish forks and meat forks and salad forks and arcane pickle knives, and sit back to see if a guest floundered or swam.

When Jonathan sat down next to the girl at the dining table, she nudged him and nodded towards his napkin. He looked at her napkin spread out on her lap, and quickly placed his own upon his knees.

'A glass of wine, Jonathan?' the mother asked. 'I think young people should be educated to drink properly, don't you?' She indicated to the father to pour him a glass.

'He doesn't like it,' the girl said.

'I'll try some,' he said, giving her a gentle kick under the table.

The mother stood up to bring in the first course, walking a little crookedly into the kitchen.

'Cigarette?' offered the father from the opposite end of the table.

'No thanks. I don't smoke,' said Jonathan.

'I'll have one,' said Jane, who was twelve, a bud flowered. She was already taller than the girl, with strong, adult features, vivid and disconcerting.

The father tossed the cigarette packet and a box of matches down towards Jane's end of the table.

'I'll have one too,' said Paul, and before long they were a little puffing family, the dining room hung with smoke, the brightness of the sun banished.

The mother reappeared bearing a tray. On each plate was the perfect head of a globe artichoke, as unbreachable as a pine cone, a culinary assault course. The girl felt something inside herself drop. It might have been the collapse of the last remaining hope that her mother would show mercy.

Jonathan picked up his knife and fork.

'Best use your fingers, sweetheart,' the mother said.

Jonathan Jamieson sobbed when the girl gave him up for the shadow lover and all the cruel lovers to come.

She was not troubled by the fact that she was a cruel lover herself, for she was a romantic girl who believed that somewhere there was a lover she would one day reach, a perfect lover she did not yet know but whom she would recognise at once.

THIRTY-ONE

The flowered bud, wrestled

WHO WOULD GUESS THAT WRESTLING a flowered bud to the floor would feel so ecstatic? Jane and I were always arguing, every morning at breakfast, every morning on the way to school, every afternoon when we got home. Our mother regularly grabbed us by the scruffs of our necks and threw us out the door, locking it behind us. 'Come back when you can be civil to each other,' she shouted, which might have been amusing in other circumstances. Did our mother even know what civility was?

One afternoon I heard Jane on the phone, when I wished to use the phone to call my deflowerer. She was fourteen, with bigger bosoms than me.

'So, like, I said to him, like, what do you mean? What do you think's going on?'

I listened to her for as long as I could, then I went to stand in front of her. In those days we had a hallstand next to the front door, with a little seat on it. The style, I think, was called 'colonial', and our newly built house was furnished in reproduction colonial style. Jane was sitting there on our reproduction colonial hallstand, crossing her long tanned legs, which she admired as she spoke.

'Hang up now,' I said. 'I've got to call Jonathan.'

She ignored me. 'Like, it's not as if I even looked at him! Like, *really*.' She drawled the last word out as if it were a long piece of chewing gum on a string between her fingers. *Reeaally*. I couldn't stand it.

'Hang up,' I repeated.

She ignored me.

'If you don't hang up right this second, I'll hit you.'

She did not respond.

I thumped her in the head, not hard.

'You bitch!' she shouted, leaping on me.

We were on the floor, wrestling, rolling over and over, scratching, pulling hair. Rhett raced up, barking, biting my assailant where he could, my dog, my champion, my hero.

'Get off me!' she cried, to the dog or to me, I don't know which. For I was pummelling her hard now.

'You fucking bitch!' Jane cried when she finally broke free, her hair hanging over her face, a red scratch down her flawless cheek.

To this day I can remember the satisfaction of that moment.

THIRTY-TWO

The shadow lover

CONSIDER THE URETHRA. HARDLY MORE than an inch long, that workmanlike tube of transport leading from the sac of the bladder, discharging urine from the body. In women, a straightforward, simple device; in men, an anxious site which doubles as a venue for ejaculation.

Consider the urethra, linked to the female somatic nervous system, so that occasionally too much sex causes it too much excitement, making it retreat in shocked affront like a Victorian maiden, red, inflamed.

When the girl, now a young woman, turns nineteen she abandons Jonathan Jamieson with his caramel-coloured skin and takes a lover as mysterious as love.

For five long years she is jealous of a shadow, a dark, unknowable shape she cannot see.

The shadow lover is very clever, a PhD candidate who studied at Yale. Not many Australian students studied internationally in those days and among his friends he has a certain cachet. He has a name, a perfectly ordinary name, but to the romantic girl he is nameless, faceless, a superior, supernatural being of inhuman dimensions.

But wait! How did the girl travel so quickly from a tender-hearted deflowerer who held her with a kind and steady hold to a shadow lover too dark to see? How did she move through time, blink, blink, loved one minute and loveless the next?

Oh, those days. Those days in which jealousy was supposed to be dead. Those days in which you were supposed to share your lovers like a box of chocolates, and marriage and monogamy were considered vanquished.

The shadow lover swears to the loveless girl that he is seeing no-one else. He suggests, too, that she get psychiatric help because she is mad. She knows she is mad: on some nights, alone in her shared student house waiting for him to come, she scratches her fingernails up her legs, up her arms, up the body that he does not honour. Welts spring up, drops of blood.

Here is what the body knows: that misery causes the blood to grow sluggish, the breath to stink, the eyes to lose the capacity to register any face that is not his. Once, in the deepest period of her misery, her body loses its ability to wake up. Night after night her somatic nervous system tries to send her a message but every morning she awakes drenched in her own piss.

Sometimes the shadow lover says: 'It doesn't mean anything.'

Sometimes he says: 'Look, Deb, there are women and children dying in Rhodesia. Pol Pot is murdering his own people. Your little agonies are nothing.'

Sometimes he says: 'I don't give a fuck what you think. I'll sleep with whoever I want.'

The romantic girl tries very hard not to focus on her little agonies but the whole world distorts itself into the dimensions of a shadow. She tries hypnotism and drinking and yoga and drugs and other lovers and consoling dreams of suicide. She tries thinking about Pol Pot's poor murdered souls but this only makes her feel more wretched and ashamed. Every face that is not his face is no face at all, and every room without him in it is empty.

Thirty years later, she cannot remember what the shadow lover looked like. She knows he is still alive because her friends sometimes come across him. He lectures on the American novel at a well-known university but the woman knows that even if she were to meet him face to face she would be unable to make him out.

The image beneath the glass was always obscured from her, even before the shadow lover became a memory, even before time's invisible transport moved him away, because certain lovers are, from the first, impossible to see.

THIRTY-THREE

Claudette

JUST BEFORE THE YOUNG WOMAN meets the shadow lover she gets her first car. A certain Renault 12, white, name of Claudette, with a slight dent in the back bumper bar, which spins along roads with freedom in its engine. Its steering wheel is perfectly shaped, thin, hard, with little ridges, and her fingers feel happy wrapped around it. Unlike her trapped mother, unlike Super Nan with an enraged husband who happened to be a big fellow with a gun, unlike her sad relative Mademoiselle Joubert, the young woman can climb into her own car and drive away.

THIRTY-FOUR

Feet

NOW THE FEET. THE FEET serve as the foundation of the body, as the engine of propulsion, the means by which we traverse the pathless lines of the world.

Mountaineers believe that some climbers have an artist's eye for the most beautiful routes up difficult peaks. Such climbers instinctively understand the aesthetic appeal of a particular route up a mountain, allowing their feet to follow their eyes, trusting them to find the most beautiful way forward.

Achilles died from a wound to the heel, the only vulnerable spot on his body, a spot made by his mother's fingers as she first dangled him into the Styx, the river of the underworld, and then held him over the fire that burnt away his mortality.

Like my hands, my feet are small, often sweaty, the confessors of my body's discomfort. High-arched, blunt of toe, as wide as paddles, they have walked Corsican beaches, the streets of Copenhagen, impressing themselves upon the grass outside the back door of a flat in Old South Head Road, Sydney. They have danced in stockinged feet or barefoot, they have danced in high-heeled shoes, in Doc Martens and in satin slippers, performing acrobatic feats of uncertain grace, revolving around and around dance floors and living rooms and kitchens, scarcely seeming to touch the turning earth.

Once I saw a foot-washing ceremony in a small stone church on the Greek island of Kythera. It was Maundy Thursday, the sky a peerless blue, and an old priest was carefully washing a parishioner's feet, one at a time. In some cities of America there are churches that make it their business to give the city's poorest a hot, nourishing meal, but only after volunteers have washed their dirty feet.

I also washed my new husband's feet. I wished to show gratitude, to render transparent my lover's boundless heart.

One morning, not long before my fiftieth year approached, I felt a sharp pain in my right foot and looked down. Sprouting from the soft fleshy part at the inner side of my foot, immediately below the big toe, a bunion had appeared. Overnight, my foot suddenly looked as my father's had when he was an old man, misshapen, buckled, ready to walk towards the last of its numbered days.

THIRTY-FIVE

Kiss me, Steph

WHAT A TALE THE BODY tells. What a repository of kisses and sighs!

The tiny crooked scar on the elastic bridge of flesh between the thumb and forefinger of my left hand, from an accidental slip of Steph's Swiss Army knife that silver day when we shucked oysters on the beach. Steph, who remained long after Nina Payne and her pale, easily bruised skin were forgotten.

Steph and I driving off in Claudette on a whim one silver morning instead of going to lectures, Steph lying on the back seat, singing her heart out, the tips of her brown toes sticking out the window.

Steph, who walked on the very tips of her brown toes. Even from a great distance her gait was immediately recognisable, a light, springy step, as if she were skipping. Steph brought her guitar that bright flowering day and cracked us up doing Tiny Tim impersonations. She made friends with a fisherman, a surfer, a wet dog. She made friends with everyone because Steph was made for friendship. She was always helping girls leave their boyfriends, or supporting them if they did not, or else watering the plants and feeding the animals and doing the banking or the shopping for the many friends who knew they could count on her. Once she took around meals to our staunch friend Ro's ailing mother; Ro did not want to go herself, because her mother was a battleaxe. The first thing the battleaxe said to Steph as she laid out the dinner was that she did not care for macaroni. Then she asked if Steph could work out a menu in advance for her approval. 'And I always eat at seven. On the dot.' The battleaxe had a patrician English accent.

Steph, who I once tried to kiss. It was the heady days of women's liberation and being a radical lesbian was a political statement; that is, feminism was the theory and lesbianism was the practice. Steph, who in my arms was surprisingly tiny, Steph at a gay bar with me, which was full of lesbian separatists.

As soon as I kissed Steph, she started to giggle. And then I started to giggle too, because kissing her felt all wrong, like attempting to tongue-kiss Miss Meow.

THIRTY-SIX

Justine Gervais

BUT HOW I LONGED TO kiss the lips of Justine Gervais!

I remember the fullness of Justine Gervais's bottom lip, the plump curve at the centre, the bow of her upper lip, and the exact way the upper and lower lips crumpled into a smile.

Her head was always slightly dipped, as if she were shy and forever looking up through her lashes. But that can't be right, that can't be true, for Justine Gervais was a leader of women, the first who told me that it was a political act to sleep with a woman. Justine Gervais had something to sell, a polemic, a dream, a bright inflamed future, a whole new way of being a woman.

So Justine Gervais could not have looked up at me through pretty lashed eyes, like a coquette. She probably looked up with a quizzical expression, a challenge no less, with her usual clever, appraising way of addressing the world. She had a naturally furrowed brow, hooded dark eyes, a fierce look, as if she was born ready to burn at the stake.

Justine Gervais, in her Levi's 501s and her T-shirt bearing the words *Dare to struggle, dare to win!*, her upper body bending across a table to make a point. She had olive skin, the finest composition of bones, a natural elegance. I watched her at university gatherings speaking out in favour of abortion rights or the right to march or solidarity with the Chilean people against Pinochet. Once she wore a second-hand ivory-coloured chiffon blouse. The sun was shining through the window behind her at such an angle that it made her blouse see-through, revealing the outline of a single perfect breast. I saw the tip of a nipple, aroused, erect, because it was the passionate discourse of politics that sexually moved her.

Justine Gervais had a girlfriend, a plain, pug-nosed lesbian who had never known a man. Justine Gervais had known lots of men, leaving a trail of broken-hearted lovers all over the city, university lecturers and fellow students, student leaders, Communist Party officials and trade unionists. They loved her for her perfect breasts, for her pure, political heart. *No socialist liberation without women's liberation!* she shouted in the street, and, *What do we want? Free and safe abortion! When do we want it? Now!* And everyone who heard her, men and women, sighed with longing.

I watched her dancing with her girlfriend at the gay bar filled with lesbian separatists. I was drunk, consumed with yearning, as if I had never known what desire was. I watched her swaying, rolling, twisting, her elegant limbs moving in a way which revealed how they might move in the act of love. Justine Gervais arched her long French–Australian neck and I glimpsed how she might look as the brief joyous throb arrived, that mysterious, timeless moment with no past or future, upon which marriages, careers, religions and kingdoms have risen and fallen.

Weeks later, in the kitchen at a party, she kissed me. 'You're gorgeous,' she said, falling towards me. Her mouth was soft, ridiculously so, as if there was nothing to it, as if her lips were nothing but vapour.

I was twenty years old, still in thrall to the shadow lover, and I had not touched another female body since Nina Payne's.

I did not know what to do with the weight of Justine Gervais in my arms. She felt dangerous, like live electricity, like an unexploded bomb. I did not want her, not really, not then, not like that. I wanted her in my head, as a dream, as an idea, not as a flesh-and-blood woman.

'Do you want to come back to my place?' she asked and I blushed.

'What about your girlfriend?' I said.

She laughed. 'Mandy's cool,' she said. 'She's staying at Lou's.'

I disengaged my body.

I took a step backwards.

'Ah, listen . . .' I said.

'Look,' I said. 'This is . . . well, it's just that I've got a boyfriend.'

Justine Gervais smiled. 'I know.' But she must have seen something else, because she stepped forward and took my hand in hers, raising it to her blazing, tied-to-the-stake face.

'When you're ready,' she said. 'I'll wait.'

·

Justine Gervais, are you waiting still?

Are you waiting with your crumpled lips in Sydney or London or Rome?

Most likely you forgot about waiting.

But my remembering arms have never forgotten the delicious shock of holding you.

THIRTY-SEVEN

A bridge

THE HAPPY DAY ARRIVED WHEN the young woman flew away. It was a long day, because the young woman did not stop flying until she reached the other side of the world.

She was flying from the turban, from the magic carpet and the beautiful sister, from the lover who was a shadow. She could feel the clutch of fingers desperate to catch the heel of her foot as she took off.

She fetched up in London, at the big old house of staunch Ro's favourite aunt, Sheila, in Ealing. Amazingly, Sheila was the sister of the battleaxe, who had abandoned England with her young family many years before. Sheila was nothing like the battleaxe or indeed anything like Ro, who was a great hulk of a woman, large-bummed, rolling. Sheila was tall and skinny with a long, intelligent face like Leonard Woolf, with prominent teeth, and was a leading scholar of English place names. It was her passionate belief that names drawn from the landscape were not trivial or accidental, but navigational and critical. She told the girl that Anglo-Saxons once had more than forty words to describe hills, from the slant of their slopes to the particular trees that grew upon them, almost as many words as the Inuit had for snow.

Sheila had three daughters, tall and skinny with long, intelligent faces like their mother and their own academic fields which absorbed them. One was a botanist, one a linguist, the third taught mathematics. Each daughter lived with a restrained, softly spoken lover who treated her kindly and with respect. One evening Sheila confided that the lover of the middle daughter had that morning spoken harshly to the daughter, and Sheila and her daughters were giddy from shock.

It was not long after anarchy had arrived in the UK, when the IRA was blowing up members of the British aristocracy and the grave-diggers and garbagemen were on strike, not long after the Iron Lady had moved into Downing Street. The twentieth century was twenty-odd years from its end, the historical process was in full swing, but the young woman's grasp on Marxist theory was shaky. The only thing that welled up in her was personal, for like everyone she experienced history from the feet up. She was no good at analysis; you might even say her methodology was suspect.

London had no coffee shops except for one or two in Soho, which was still lined with strip clubs, the haunt of prostitutes and their clients. The first thing the young woman did after she unpacked her backpack and unrolled her sleeping bag was take the Tube to The Strand, where she walked up the stairs of a big old building and into a women's liberation meeting. They were planning a Reclaim the Night march through the streets of Soho and so the young woman strode out with them, her denim overalls festooned with badges, her hair cropped against her skull, reclaiming the street, the night, the furthest outposts of her own skin.

The second thing she did was go to see her friend Steph. Steph was living in Paris with an Arab boy. Nasser was twenty-one years old, like them. He was from Jordan and made sculptures from the flotsam of the streets, working as a cook in a Tunisian restaurant at night. Steph and Nasser lived under the eaves of a crumbling once-grand house in the fourteenth arrondissement, in a cramped *chambre de bonne* with a gas ring and a sink, and a shared toilet down the hall. Its saving grace was a series of beautiful little arched windows through which the roofs and chimneys and balconies of Paris were framed like a painting.

The windows had shutters they usually closed at night—except on those nights when the moon was full. 'Ladies and gentlemen,' Steph said, standing beneath the shutters holding her arms aloft like a television hostess. '*Je vous présente Paris par nuit.*'

And there it was, Paris, gleaming, hardly real.

'I always wanted to live in a garret,' Steph said, holding Nasser's black head against her chest and stroking his hair. They were smoking hash through a hookah of porcelain, blue-beaded glass and brass, their limbs sprawled on hand-woven patterned rugs. Although he was only twenty-one, Nasser wore a silk cravat.

Steph had a *carte de séjour* and a job teaching English, but she was hot-hearted and impulsive like the young woman, and occasionally forgot to turn up to classes. She became overly involved in her students' home lives and one afternoon appeared at the *chambre de bonne* with a sobbing, soft-faced Algerian boy whose father had beaten him.

'He can't stay here!' said Nasser.

'Yes, he can,' said Steph. 'At least until we find him somewhere else.'

He slept on the floor next to the young woman and sobbed discreetly all night.

When Steph was sacked, she persuaded the young woman to go busking with her on the Île Saint-Louis. Steph played guitar and she and the young woman sang a passable rendition of 'Chuck E's in Love'. Sometimes that summer, if the stars were in an auspicious position and the two friends felt a lyricism moving in them, they opened their mouths and joy flowed effortlessly from them.

So it was with a song in her mouth that the young woman found her next object lover. Her eyes found it first, the graceful shape of the Pont Marie, its radiant arches rising up from the darkness of the Seine. She had supposed herself tired of beauty; the soft white statues of the Louvre made her seasick, the endless rows of paintings caused her to feel faint. The sight of the bridge restored her to beauty, satisfying every idea of beauty she did not know until that moment she possessed.

Beauty enters first through the eyes and the young woman rushed towards it, hungry for its touch. There was a gap between her as the observer and the bridge as the observed and she craved to close it, to make the distance between her and beauty disappear.

The pearly stones of the Pont Marie were warm from the sun. Under her hand the stones pulsed like flesh and she was not surprised to find when she leant against it that it carried the heat of a body. It had a heartbeat, a hum, a memory of all the accumulated breaths that had breathed upon it. Its stones were barnacled with ghosts, with the collective wishes of the unrecorded vanished. For a moment the young woman was certain that if she listened hard enough the tide of souls who had passed across might break through the fabric of the perished world to fill the air with sound.

The bridge had a mystical beauty, unadorned, like the plainest whitewashed Greek church. All along its sides were empty niches, waiting perhaps for the relics of a saint. The bridge's beauty was sacred, and set up in the young woman's heart a little festival of gratitude. Standing at its centre, her feet firm on its breathing stones, she felt exultant, every cell in her body roused and ready. She felt that at last she had entered the house of beauty; it had materialised, and was real.

THIRTY-EIGHT

Even dead husbands must be counted

SUPER NAN SAID THAT WHEN she lived in Orange, Rene Ferguson (short for Irene) was on her way to her husband Ted's funeral when she was killed by his coffin. The marriage had not been happy, Super Nan confided, and it was bloody typical of him, excuse the French.

'Anyway'—Super Nan always spiced her stories liberally with 'anyway'—'on the way to the cemetery to bury the old b, the hearse was hit from the rear by another car,' Super Nan said. 'The coffin in the back slammed straight into poor Rene's head.'

Isn't it right that sooner or later the body acknowledges the slam of the coffin, the fatal wound to the back of the head? Love lives in the body and when love dies the body is the first to know. My husband wanted to make love to me after I had ceased to love him, but my body had already felt the slam of the coffin.

THIRTY-NINE

France

FRANCE WAS THE YOUNG WOMAN'S America, her new-found land, not so much a place as an idea. It was her landscape, hardly a country, more a sensation. A place of white roads, blossoming light, scarlet geraniums, of avenues of plane trees planted by kings to inscribe their power upon rural space.

The young woman travelled to Corsica, to Fontainebleau, to the Breton fishing village of Pornic and small stone villages high in the Pyrenees. She watched the tips of the vine leaves turn russet in Fitou in late September and walked through chestnut forests in the Aude with Steph, Nasser and a group of French friends, searching for wild mushrooms. When they found the ceps, the head of each one was fleshy, pink, swollen, resembling the glans of a tumescent penis stripped of its foreskin.

·

The young woman secretly cherished a foolish, romantic idea that being French was more interesting than being Australian, but would never have admitted it.

'Where are your roots?' Nasser asked her one night. 'Mine are in Jordan.'

She thought for a moment. She loved Australia but she also loved France. She wondered if she might be like a plant whose roots do not travel down but sideways.

In France she was someone else. She was a girl whose limbs were free, with carte blanche to fill herself in. The words on her tongue were different and she felt her old self slipping away. For the first time she began to wonder how language built identity, how it had a magical ability to transform existence.

She grew her hair and had it cut in an asymmetrical shape against her jaw, and powdered her eyes in shadow. She practised French and was amazed at the nuances of words. At a mutual acquaintance's *vernissage* she met Horatia Craig, named for Admiral Lord Nelson because she was born on Trafalgar Day. An Englishwoman of Scottish descent, she lived in a large airy flat on the rue Saint-Jacques. There were fifty years between Horatia and the young woman but no gap.

Horatia was rich, and happened to be a lesbian of the old school. She had known Janet Flanner and Djuna Barnes and found the modern-day political lesbian, shorn of adornment, distasteful. 'In life one should always seek the beautiful,' she said. Horatia had good bones and dressed in exquisitely cut clothes, her silver hair a shining cap, her mouth carefully lipsticked. She lived platonically with a dour-looking Frenchwoman named Monique. As far as the young woman could tell, Monique served as a kind of lady's maid to Horatia.

'I am not a lesbian,' Horatia said. 'I just loved dear lost Beth.'

It was thrilling, knowing beautiful rich old lesbians in Paris. It was thrilling, sitting in Horatia's richly furnished room, the windows open to the rue Saint-Jacques, being fed pastel macaroons from Ladurée, the palest pistachio green, the faintest rose, a jewellery box of colours.

While Horatia did not actively flirt with the young woman, she admitted to a little frisson. 'One must take love where one finds it,' she said. She had lived long enough to see that each life had a shape, and liked to watch the way a young life unfurled, which parts blossomed and which parts atrophied, unwatered, unfed. Whenever Horatia said goodbye to the young woman, she kissed her on each cheek, once, twice, and then again, four kisses. 'We are intimates now, my dear,' she said.

The young woman never left Horatia's company without feeling that her understanding of life had previously been too small, and that the world was larger, and more promising, than she'd thought.

But at night, in the cramped *chambre de bonne*, the young woman dreamed only of the shadow lover. She would return to him after she landed home again, because the compelling drive to repeat the past is encoded in the cells of certain young women, despite feminist and Marxist theory, despite the example of Miss Horatia Craig and history's finest lessons.

FORTY

Words

MY TONGUE LOVES TO CURL itself around a French word, to feel my lips push out into a sensual pout because French words sit forward in the mouth, well past the fat roll of tongue at the back of the throat and down and over the slippy pointed tip which meets the teeth.

A word can be as delicious upon the tongue as dissolving chocolate. My tongue loves to roll and dip around words, exotic words and plain words, foreign words and English words, strange words and familiar. A word is a kingdom, a key, a clue, a word is a thing to savour and roll upon the tongue, and if we are lucky sometimes words are all that are left to us.

At ninety-five, Nana Elsie still ruled over a realm of words. Towards the end I sat with her and held her hand even though she had lost her lips and forgotten who she was. Her words were random, mysterious, floating. 'The clothes are burning,' she might say, or 'Beautiful brown' or 'She's a good cup.'

Once, in a rare moment of lucidity, she said, 'If I gave you a thousand pounds, would you take me home?'

Nana Elsie and her radiance appeared to dwell between this world and the next, in the slippage between them, where life meets death and where time is rendered eternal.

FORTY-ONE

Words in her fingers

IN PARIS THE YOUNG WOMAN began to formulate a plan. She wanted to hold words in her fingers as well as in her mouth, to move words this way and that.

Steph knew the manager of an English-language bookshop, who knew someone who knew someone else, and so it was that the young woman found herself working part-time in Shakespeare and Co, the famous bookstore on rue de la Bûcherie owned by the eccentric American, George Whitman. George sometimes came down from his room above the shop dressed in his pyjamas, his hair wild, to shout winningly at customers. 'Look sharp, Deborah,' he once shouted. She was shocked to find he knew her name.

At Shakespeare and Co she met the owner of a small English press, who needed a proofreader. And so she began proofreading and copyediting, reading the pages of manuscripts, working carefully with her fingers and eyes on tiny black marks against white. It was pernickety, detailed work, requiring concentrated and discerning effort. She imagined it to resemble the art of lace-making, stitching everything perfectly together as if with a very fine needle.

Sometimes she found the work a chore, her brain anxious and trying too hard, and then she stumbled and made the mistakes that she feared. Soon she recognised that if she allowed her eyes and fingers to act instinctively, the work became fluid and easy.

She fell in love with the laws of form, the satisfactions of order, with the illusory human notion that everything could be perfected. Sometimes the fingers who loved her thought they knew everything. She was still an unfortunate romantic girl who wanted everything explained.

In wielding her needle, she came across a word she believed described herself. It was a French word, *métèque*, meaning foreigner or stranger and, more pejoratively, wog. It came from the ancient Greek word *metic*, which referred to those in the Hellenic cities who were stateless.

The definition of *métèque* she liked best of all was 'suspicious wanderer'. She took to signing the letters she wrote to Ro back in Sydney with her new favoured initials, SW, for Suspicious Wanderer.

FORTY-TWO

Heavenly sleep

LISTEN TO THIS: IN A global survey of some twelve thousand five hundred souls, almost sixty percent admitted they preferred a good night's sleep to a night of magnificent sex.

In nine out of ten western countries, men and women confessed that sex was all very well, but sleep was essential. Only horny Canadians preferred sex to sleep.

I lost my ability to sleep after the birth of my son. I became an incurable insomniac, listening for each newborn breath. I was his guard, and for a while I thought I had to breathe for him. By the time I discovered that I did not, it was too late, and I was tipped forever from sleep's rosy arms into wakeful vigilance.

For many years my bed, like my body, was my son's playground and his kingdom. I surrendered to him, willingly and grudgingly, because by then I knew that ambivalence lived beside me and in me, inhabiting everything, even that unbreakable watchfulness between mother and son. By then I was no longer a romantic.

When my son was a growing boy, long and stretched and fatless, his legs like gnawed chicken bones as mine had once been, I loved to watch him sleeping.

He tucked himself into sleep as if into the most comfortable of beds. He locked himself tight into its furthest corner, sealed into sweet oblivion. At the time he liked being asleep more than anything else. When he was twelve, thirteen, fourteen, his voice not yet broken, his body invisibly knitting itself into new adult dimensions, he slept for hours and hours.

He was like a newborn again, except that it was his adult self being born. He was lost, happy, found, away, in a beautiful place of his own making. His face was as composed as a mask and only occasionally would his eyelids flutter with a dream.

Now, my vigilant nights have a particular sweetness, my long-ago moments coming again in the stillness of the hour. My body's memories crowding in, my endless loves, once more awake.

FORTY-THREE

Coffee

THAT SUMMER IN PARIS BEGAN in one single, gleaming day. One evening the Suspicious Wanderer went to bed with the sky starless, unseen clouds dense with rain. In the morning she opened the shutters to a glittering new world. Sunlight polished windows and rinsed the streets, shutters and doors and windows were open everywhere, flowers had bloomed overnight. She thought she heard laughter.

She looked down at herself, dressed in one of Nasser's oversized T-shirts, shrugged, then grabbed her bag and the house keys. 'Paris, here I come,' she said, running down the circular stairs two, three at a time. The old stairs with their narrow wooden steps and thin, curved wooden handrails never failed to lift her heart and they lifted it now, high, high, higher.

On the street everyone looked happy. It was already hot, and she wasn't wearing anything beneath her T-shirt. The cotton rubbed satisfactorily against her high pink-tipped breasts, still unsuckled.

She strode purposefully down Avenue du Maine, past Metro Alésia, past the beautiful creamy stone church on the corner, past scooters and markets and old ladies with shopping baskets and students with cigarettes and scarves.

'I will stop at the first café I like the look of,' she said to herself, and by this she meant one that faced exactly the right way into the sun, with a table and chair situated exactly in the position she wished it. It drove Steph and Nasser mad, her insistence on choosing exactly the right café, with exactly the right chair at the right table.

'Just bloody sit down, will you?' Steph was likely to say.

'*S'il te plaît*, Madame Marie-Antoinette,' said Nasser.

But now she was alone. She saw a café up ahead, one facing the right way into the sun. She sat down. Immediately a waiter, wearing the obligatory white Parisian waiter's apron, came up. '*Mademoiselle?*' She ordered and sat back, happy.

She recommends that anyone suffering *tristesse* drink one cup of well-made coffee, slowly and deliberately, savouring the milk, the heat, the roast. Savour the flavour upon the tongue, the entrance into the body. Think of your great good fortune in being able to sit and drink a cup of coffee with your own two hands, of the pleasures of being able to taste it. You don't have to be in Paris to feel blessed: Burwood, Sydney, will do, or Brookline, Massachusetts, or the far reaches of unattractive Leytonstone.

Is there anything more seductive than the smell of coffee beans rising to the nostrils? That rich, deep aroma, conviviality made manifest, the brown, ripe smell of harvest. The woman remembers once carrying freshly roasted coffee beans home on a bus in Sydney and how the smell rose to her nostrils, which suddenly struck her as the organ through which God breathes, in that she and everyone else on the bus breathed in as one the same rich dark scent.

'Lovely, isn't it?' said the woman sitting next to her.

'Divine,' said the elderly woman across the aisle.

The bus rattled along with everyone on it sharing the same beautiful smell of coffee beans; the smell of shared confidences, of friendship and of pleasure.

Later, the woman drank the most perfect cup of coffee of her life, not in a nameless café in a street somewhere off the Avenue du Maine, or in a café in Melbourne, but in a room in the hills of Umbria. The steamed milk, the coffee beans, the ritual of making the cup of coffee to bring to the table, all combined to make her feel lucky to be able to drink it, with a tongue in her mouth to taste and two hands with which to hold the cup, a stomach in which to catch the earth's bounteous spill.

But on that long-ago summer morning in Paris the young woman had not yet been to Umbria. She was happy to find herself sitting alone on the first bright morning of summer in the lucky western world, feeling her unbound breasts, her free toes, the sun, her lover, warm on her skin and the wash of freshly made coffee in her mouth.

Three men in one day

IF THE SUSPICIOUS WANDERER EVER thought that flying away from the turban, the magic carpet and the beautiful sister would rid her of them for good, she soon realised her mistake.

When she returned to Sydney she found that the sister had grown even more beautiful, the mother more drunk, the father on his magic carpet even further away with his endless maps and horizons. The poor brother had long since stepped onto that drinking path which would lead him to an early death. The dog, Rhett, was arthritic, blind, a creature so reduced that it took him a few minutes to understand that it was her, returned, and to consequently thump his patchy old tail against the floor. The very next day the mother took him to the vet to have him put down, as if she had timed this occasion expressly for the young woman to witness. 'It was a mercy,' she reported afterwards. 'He just faded away.' Miss Meow had disappeared some months before.

•

She was back in the arms of the shadow lover, but she was also not really back. Even as she kissed his ghostly lips, her spirit was away.

She slept with a film-maker many years older than her, who wanted to film them fucking. She said yes, but she meant to say no. Afterwards she wondered if the film-maker had wiped the film as he promised.

Sometimes she wonders if somewhere in the world today there is a film of a young woman, recently turned twenty-two, looking as if she is not sure what she is doing, if she is here or there, asleep or awake.

She slept with a sad-faced boy at a party because the shadow lover was at the party too, except that she could not find him. She searched every room, the front yard and the back, before finally glimpsing him down the lane behind the backyard of the house. He was fucking a girl against a fence and the Suspicious Wanderer quickly ran inside and grabbed the hand of the sad-faced boy and led him to the nearest bedroom.

She slept with an Italian hairdresser with the splendid name of Leonardo della Francesca, who came on her stomach because he did not trust women. He said all women were manipulative by nature and every woman wanted a husband. He would not put it past one to trick him into marriage by accidentally-on-purpose becoming pregnant.

·

One day she inadvertently slept with all three. This is how it happened: one evening she went to bed with the older film-maker, a sensual and lazy lover who lapped at her lips and between her legs. In the morning they made love again, still slippery from the night before. Every girl in the whole world was on the pill then, and no-one used condoms.

Walking home from the film-maker's house she met the sad-faced boy. He promised to cook her lunch and afterwards they spent two gentle hours on his Indian bedspread, beneath a poster of Prime Minister Malcolm Fraser printed with the words: *For the man who said life wasn't meant to be easy MAKE LIFE IMPOSSIBLE.*

When she reached home she ran a bath and soaked pleasurably for an hour. She put on her favourite nightie and crawled between sheets freshly washed the day before. Luxuriating in the full splay of her limbs, her toes flexed against the top sheet tucked tight into the end of the bed, she sighed. She considered her body honoured, even worshipped.

She was almost asleep when she heard a knock at the door. It was Leonardo della Francesca, with a bottle of Asti Spumante and a dozen red roses. *'Ciao, bella,'* he said.

She knew that if Leonardo della Francesca knew there had been two men before him he would turn on his heel. Yet she also knew as she took his hand that she felt free and alive. In those days she still calculated her worth on how many men wished to sleep with her. She had no idea how to calculate her own value so she put herself up for market valuation, not knowing the fallibility of the marketplace or the fickleness of the laws of supply and demand.

'No coming on my stomach tonight,' she instructed Leonardo della Francesca as she took his hand and led him to what she thought was her triumphant bed.

FORTY-SEVEN

Skin

THIS HOUSE OF SKIN, THIS empire of net in which I am captured, how well it has held me. Full of breath, blood, cellular intelligence, its own plans. All my stories written on it, my skin memories, the tiny crack just below the hairline where my father failed to catch me when I jumped from a tree into his catchless arms, the white stripe on the back of my thumb from a cut from a shard of porcelain, the scar high up on my hip where I burnt myself while ironing naked, my attention having wandered into an erotic daydream of the dissolute lover who made my stomach lurch whenever I saw him, as if travelling too fast in a car over an unexpected hill.

The skin tags scattered around my neck, soft brown nubbles of flesh, round. When my son was learning to speak, he loved nothing better than trying to pick one. "Tana,' he said, short for sultana, which he imagined they were, since he could see no reason why my plentiful body, the source of everything he needed and desired, should not grow sultanas.

The first lover I slept with after I lost my husband sometimes traced his fingers around my necklace of sultanas. 'Fruits of the body,' he said, like a poet, and I was struck by how closely this matched my baby son's description.

Ro, with a battleaxe for a mother, betrayed by her own net of skin. Staunch Ro, firm friend to Steph and me, felled at forty, well before her mother the battleaxe, who died comfortably in her bed at ninety-three. A tiny mole on the skin, so infinitely capable!

Ro, that great hulk of a woman, with an enormous bum that sprouted straight from the middle of her back like an African woman's, that bum which rolled impressively when she walked, each gigantic buttock apparently independent of the other. 'There she blows,' Steph used to say fondly as she approached, and indeed our Ro resembled a great seaworthy vessel, unsinkable.

Sometimes, even now, I lift the phone to ring her.

Sometimes, even now, I want someone to tell me where the dead go.

FORTY-EIGHT

The lover who fell in love with desire

BACK IN AUSTRALIA THE SUSPICIOUS Wanderer no longer felt at home. She had entered that parlous state, the terrain of the liminal, one foot in night and one foot in day. Her body was in Australia but her heart was in France, which was not her home either.

She stayed away from her family as politely as she could. She was still busy abasing herself at the hands of the shadow lover, who was telling her that she was not clever or anywhere near as beautiful as her sister. She was busy sleeping with as many lovers as possible, with as many glamorous and feckless men as she could find.

In between sleeping with men and abasing herself at the hands of the shadow lover she was busy sewing words. She was happiest of all when her fingers were swift and acting, taken up with the task of mending the word-lace. She found work as an editor on a reference book about gardens, and found beauty and satisfaction in equal parts in tidying up the scraps, the last loose threads of black upon white. You could say her fingers were searching on her behalf for a more satisfactory mode of being.

One morning a young landscape gardener came into the office. He had only ever written one or two articles before, and the Suspicious Wanderer's boss asked her to oversee the writing of an article she had commissioned. The landscape gardener, who was called Nick, was much the same age as the young woman, with an attractive looseness about his person.

That winter in Sydney was the coldest in sixty years. Snow reached the Blue Mountains, even Hornsby, and could be felt as a kind of vibration in the air. Frost frilled the mornings, enamelling the earth.

Throughout that famous cold winter when the young woman slept with Nick he kept a fire burning in his strange, falling-down house. He kept that fire burning all day and night in an old blackened pot-belly stove he had rigged up, held by wire to one gaping wall at the side of the house. It was like camping, staying at Nick's, his bed a mattress and a few sleeping bags on the floor, in a part of the house without walls. At night they lay with their faces turned up to the trembling air, looking at the stars. Nick wore a beanie to bed and the young woman took to wearing one too, pulled down hard over her ears because otherwise they throbbed with cold.

Nick was a wonderful kisser, and the Suspicious Wanderer loved kissing. She loved the creamy thrill of it, the closed-eyed sway. She loved the intimacy of her tongue inside another person's mouth, the tongue that moved words around, the tongue that was thick and alive and rooted deep in the floor of her mouth, and in his, muscled, pulsing.

The landscape gardener called Nick did not enter her the first night they lay together.

He kissed her instead, for one minute, and then two; for five minutes, for ten. He kissed her, standing up at first, then on the sofa, kissing and kissing. She felt for him beneath his clothes and he was already hard, straining, so she reached for his belt—but he stilled her hand. His hand moved instead to her jeans, which he unzipped, pushing aside the cotton of her underpants, his fingers diving between the creamy folds.

His touch was perfect, exact, and the wetness of his mouth, the dreamy slide of the kissing, the glide of his tongue mirrored the movement of his fingers so that before long her body was engaged in a dance of throb and sway, of rise and fall. His fingers and the lips and the sliding went on and on, for so long that she knew she would come. She had to hide her face for shame, for she could feel the flicker start up inside her, the joyous heat building and building, drawing closer with each careful stroke of his fingers. His forefinger danced, around and around, up and over. She swelled and blossomed, breathing hot into his shirt, her breath fast. She squeezed her eyes and came in a shivery wave, her blood beating.

To cover her embarrassment, the Suspicious Wanderer placed her hand upon him, still hard, trapped inside his jeans. Again the landscape gardener stopped her hand.

'Come on,' she said. 'Don't be scared.' She tugged at his belt.

'Do you want a drink?' he asked, breaking away and standing up. 'Beer? Wine?'

He tucked his shirt into his jeans and turned away.

The same thing happened the second time they slept together.

And the third.

And the fourth.

And the fifth.

And the sixth.

And the seventh.

The Suspicious Wanderer did not know the landscape gardener well enough to ask him what was happening. She hardly knew him at all and everything that they did not know about each other stood between them.

Oh, those days! Those days in which it was possible to know the intimate geography of another human body without knowing a single thing about them. It was possible to know the exact dimensions of the left nipple with a soft hair sprouting from one side, or the precise colouring of the puckered skin around a testicle, without knowing another thing about what went on within their breathing hearts. In those faraway days girls often slept with people they did not know.

·

Each time the Suspicious Wanderer and the landscape gardener came together it was the same. The first kiss, the move to the sofa, the unmade bed. In the bed on the floor beneath the freezing stars he never kissed her, never tried to enter her. They lay side by side like virgins.

'Do you understand the principles of astral navigation?' he asked her one night, long after she believed he was asleep.

'No,' she said. 'Well, sort of. Isn't that when ships steered by the stars? Before compasses?'

He did not answer. Her head was full of questions and the night was cloudless, empty but for the steering stars.

The young woman wondered if the strange young man suffered from some nameless embarrassment or a rare medical condition. She might have thought he did not want her but for the evidence of the stiff press of his penis. Perhaps he was like an Indian yogi who had learnt to withhold his pleasure for hours and hours, except that as far as the woman knew, even a yogi engaged in penetration and eventually arrived at his destination. In every other way Nick was ardent in his passion, from the embrace to the stiffened penis to the tremble of his fingers each time he approached her. Was it her fault?

Before long the Suspicious Wanderer began to grow nervous before each meeting. She grew self-conscious as he began to kiss her and the approach of his mouth felt like a test. She was filled with contradictory emotions: a desire to conquer him, to see him fall to the rapturous moment, and yet also she felt ashamed, embarrassed for herself, as if he considered her an animal, raised to do tricks for his enjoyment.

She began to withhold her pleasure, for she did not want him to witness it, and soon the kissing felt like undeclared war.

Soon the Suspicious Wanderer began to make excuses when the landscape gardener called Nick asked her to the strange, cold house. She was going out, or she had work to do, or she had the flu. He called again and again, and every time she had a reason not to go to the strange, cold house.

She finished editing his article.

After a while he ceased to call and so the young woman never got to ask the landscape gardener why he preferred the building moment over the starburst spill.

In the end she satisfied herself by supposing him to have fallen in love with desire, to have fallen in love with being perpetually held in longing's grip, with the exquisite tension of never arriving.

Sometimes now, on vigilant nights, she pictures the landscape gardener grown old, still looking up at the navigating stars.

She thinks of him lying there, the beautiful moment never arriving, never ruined, never disappointing, over. It must be sublime dwelling in that house of longing, forever poised on desire's trembling tip, before everything is wrecked.

FORTY-NINE

A dress

ONCE I FELL IN LOVE with a dress. You never forget the first dress you fall in love with, and this dress was like a template for all the dresses in the world that girls longed for, rushed down the street in, got married in, sailed away in.

It was a real dress, but it was also a dream dress, stitched from wishes. A particular shade of orangey-red, beautifully cut from the finest cotton, two elegant twists of fabric at each shoulder. Whenever I put it on I felt like a different person, a person without cares. In that dress my body relaxed and became taller, stronger, happier. I rushed, laughing, down the rue de Rivoli wearing it, holding hands with the man I was going to marry, hurrying to get to the jeweller's shop before it closed to claim the gold wedding rings engraved with our names.

I wore that perfect dress for fourteen years, until its weave wore so thin in the back the material frayed in the spot where I sat down.

FIFTY

The lover oblivion

SOME TIME AFTER FLYING HOME, between the shadow lover and the landscape gardener who fell in love with desire, between the dissolute lover who made her stomach lurch whenever she saw him and the Italian lover with the splendid name of Leonardo della Francesca, the Suspicious Wanderer's blood began to boil. It was as if her blood sought release from its prison of skin, as if everything inside her struggled to escape.

Whenever she was on a bus or a train the young woman fought a hot, vertiginous feeling that she must get off, rush away, be anywhere other than trapped where she was with a hundred eyes upon her. Her heart thrashed, her mouth grew dry, her palms ran with sweat, soaking tissues right through. All the pints of Scottish and Irish blood and her splash of French blood rose and slapped against her skin.

Paradoxically, she also felt herself to be skinless before the world. Boiling, skinless, trapped.

The Suspicious Wanderer could hardly bear to go to work. Sitting in the open-plan office trying to edit a book her body was primed for escape. Her blood and nerves and senses were on constant high alert, so that she only had to look up and chance upon a glance from a harmless passerby to find herself convulsed, flailing, jumping up and scrambling for the exit.

'It's called a panic attack,' the doctor said. 'Nothing to worry about. In fact, the worst thing you can do is worry about it. Some men find blushing very attractive.'

He wrote out a prescription for a muscle relaxant.

The Suspicious Wanderer may have been ashamed of something.

Or she may have arrived at that moment when the dizzying responsibility of being alive was revealed to her.

She understood that she was more than a brain, a set of porous lungs, a vagina. It now appeared that she was expected to become a republic of one, even a universe.

Who was in charge here?

For many months, the rush of blood to the Suspicious Wanderer's guilty face caused her to shun the company of her fellows. Soon she became phobic about going out, lest her blood begin to boil, lest everyone wonder what it was that made her so ashamed. She had witnessed no murders, no wars and no tragedies. She was not dying. Yet she appeared to be a vehicle for suffering, a conduit for the wretchedness of the world. She was more ashamed of herself than before.

Staunch Ro tried to winkle her free. 'Valium! God, Deb, you're not a 1950s housewife!'

She was living in Ro's tiny cottage in Balmain, in the miniscule second bedroom that could barely accommodate a single bed. The house seemed too small for Ro and her gigantic bottom, and for Ro's cheerful boyfriend, Mick, a hippy working temporarily at a biscuit factory because he was saving to go overseas, and who every night brought home flawed, broken biscuits.

The young woman could not stop eating flawed biscuits and soon acquired a comforting layer of protective fat.

In Ro's tiny house the Suspicious Wanderer felt lumbering, huge, and when she stood up her hair seemed almost to reach the ceiling.

Like Alice, she was too big for the house.

She appeared to be growing.

'You're looking porky,' said her father when he next saw her.

'I suggest a diet,' said her mother. Her sister smiled.

For the first time in her life it appeared the young woman could not eat anything she liked. Those well-sculpted thighs and the graceful scooped back of her girlhood were swallowed, completely gone. No-one would mistake her now for a gymnast.

It was a revelation. She noticed that being a great lump of a girl had its advantages, in that the larger she grew the more invisible she became.

She could happily live the rest of her life as a great lump of a girl, invisible, drugged, eating as many biscuits as she liked.

·

One morning, though, Ro strode over to the rubbish bin.

'This is how you save yourself,' she said, throwing away the pill bottles, the repeat prescriptions, everything that stood between the Suspicious Wanderer and panic. 'And now we are going out,' said Ro. 'Get your shoes.'

The Suspicious Wanderer followed obediently in Ro's mighty wake, sluggish. Ro was naturally commanding, preternaturally composed, possibly as a result of being the daughter of a battleaxe. A woman of few words, she was as cool-headed as the young woman was hot-headed.

'Keep up,' Ro said. 'Walking is a kind of cure. It's good for the lungs, it's good for the heart and it's especially good for the soul.'

And it was true: the young woman's feet held a flesh memory of freedom. As she placed one foot in front of the other, sadness loosed itself from her limbs, some unnamed, residual feeling that had lived within her for a long time, of being too long a lover of oblivion, too precariously balanced within its trancelike grip.

She could not keep up with Ro, but she kept her eyes fixed on her beautiful rolling bottom, leading her as it were through the swell.

But anyone who has ever loved knows the lover will not be thwarted. It did not take the young woman long to get another prescription. For many more months she continued to float in the loving arms of oblivion. Her mind did not seem to be involved, in that her addiction was more like a compulsion of the muscles, and her body wanted what it wanted, and did what it needed to do.

Valium's chemical promise quelled the boiling of her blood, placing an impenetrable wall between her body and the world. It reminded her of the single time she had snorted heroin, courtesy of a rich, pompous barrister, a friend of a friend, who was a recreational user. 'I think of heroin as an occasional treat,' the barrister said. 'Like a good bottle of Petrus.'

The young woman adored the way heroin made her feel, and how far from fear it carried her. But she was worried that she loved it too much, and never used it again.

In time in that little house in Balmain the Suspicious Wanderer became aware that the sounds of the world were increasingly muffled. Her mind was sluggish and she could not think. Everything inside her felt like it was lying down.

When her contract ended with a publisher who published cooking books she had difficulty finding more work, and when she did get jobs, publishers rarely used her a second time. Once she proofread a travel book about Australia and failed to notice that an American writer had misspelled Sydney as Sidney.

Finally the day arrived when the Suspicious Wanderer could no longer command her own fat legs.

She was walking home when her fat legs stepped off a kerb seemingly of their own accord and she was thrown backwards onto the pavement by a car.

She was not hurt because the car had barely been moving, having just taken off at a green light. But the driver got out and screamed at her for ten minutes before the Suspicious Wanderer collapsed, shaking from shock.

Up until that moment the Suspicious Wanderer had not known she did not wish to die. She had believed herself in love with oblivion but in that shocking moment she understood she was in love only with escape and not that final dark place.

She stopped swallowing Valium and flawed, broken biscuits, *pouf*, just like that.

FIFTY-ONE

The hairdresser

IS THERE ANYTHING MORE CRIMINALLY frivolous than having a hairdresser massage your scalp over a basin of warm sudsy water? Anything more indulgent than letting your body relax into the swoon of ministration under the hairdresser's healing hands? A few moments of ease in the quotidian days, with no other purpose than to soothe and pass fingers not your own through the strands of your dying hair.

FIFTY-TWO

The blind lover

HOW MANY BODIES I PLUNDERED, how many mouths I kissed before I kissed the mouth of the prince! For uncertain reasons I needed to learn many lessons involving the tongue, the hands, the ears, the belly and the fallible heart.

The moment I laid my eyes on Stephen Porter's blind eyes I knew he would become my lover. Because of the many romantic stories I had heard Super Nan tell about her blind mother, Rose—who when she was sixteen bravely sailed by herself all the way from Limerick to Australia—I had always been fascinated by blind people.

I was still with the shadow lover, in the fifth and final year of my disappearance. I was back in my body, free of drugs and biscuits, but still, still, still not free of the shadow lover.

Stephen Porter was an Honours student, majoring in French, a tremulous young man with a guide dog and a white stick, who lived down the street from Ro. She knew him vaguely and introduced us one morning as we were getting into Claudette.

'Deb's a Francophile, too,' Ro said. 'Like you she conveniently forgets France's shameful role in collaborating with the Nazis. She thinks everyone was in the French resistance.'

Stephen Porter smiled at me. 'Then we should get together, mate, and toast *la vie française*,' he said.

I watched him walk off, his white stick tapping the concrete. I was back in my body and wanted to test it.

After that first time, I met Stephen Porter several times walking down the street. He often had a small food stain on his T-shirt or a toothpaste smear around his mouth, because he had recently moved out of the family home into a house with some other students, thoughtless boys, who did not notice or care. He was frail-looking, a long-haired blond, with a fine wispy beard and an attractive way of speaking, very precise, with a slight lisp. Stephen Porter's face was vulnerable, sweet, and either his blindness had turned him gentle or else he was born that way.

When he first held me, it was with a surprising firmness. I looked into his blind eyes and he held my head between his hands and kissed me.

'I'm no different to anyone else you know, mate,' he said. 'I find girls hold very romantic views about blind men.'

'I don't!' I said and he laughed, a giggly laugh that made me laugh too.

'I know perfectly well where all your best bits are,' he said.

His eyes were a strange, indeterminate bluey-brown colour, and sometimes looked like everyone else's seeing eyes, except that one pupil was slightly larger than the other and occasionally wandered off to the outside edge of his eye. Sometimes, too, his eyes closed of their own accord, as if they were looking into the memory box inside his head. At other times his unseeing eyes looked straight into mine.

When Stephen Porter laid me on the bed it was with tenderness. He traced my form, a fingertip analysis of each curve, each crevice, each rise. His gentle mouth came to rest upon the mound between my legs, a soft suckling, bringing my own scent to my lips when he raised his head again to kiss me. My scent was caught in his moustache, a lingering fragrance. When I kissed his thin hairless chest the scent travelled with me, down to the pointed tip of his penis. We coupled gently, nuzzled, tender, arriving at our moment of sweetness in silence.

He took me to meet his family. Straight away I envied him them and wished they were mine, a measured, happy, musical family, who treated each other respectfully. The father was a metallurgist, and the mother worked with blind children, retraining after her second son was inexplicably born blind, his optic nerves having failed to develop. Sometimes they sang together around the piano, like a happy family in a children's story.

Stephen Porter's family refused to treat their blind son any differently to a sighted child. As a consequence he had repeatedly broken arms and legs, chipped a front tooth, and had given himself a white scar down the left side of his face in his quest to climb trees, shoot bows and arrows, and travel too fast on skateboards like other boys. He played the piano beautifully and the guitar badly, singing Leonard Cohen songs in his precise, high voice, transforming them entirely.

I told him Super Nan's mother had been born blind, too, but no-one knew why.

'It was a long time ago. In Ireland,' I said.

'She was lucky she wasn't tossed into the nearest well for being a witch,' he said. 'There has always been a lot of superstition about blind people.'

Not long before I slept with Stephen Porter for the last time, I asked him if he could imagine light.

'I think of it as being cream and white,' he said.

'But how can you imagine colour?' I asked. 'How do you even know what cream and white is?'

'Colour is just a concept I've picked up over the years. I think of dark as being green, or red, or black.'

I closed my eyes.

'I see everything from the inside out,' Stephen said.

As I lay on the bed with my eyes closed I tried to imagine redness. How did anyone begin to picture colour without the help of the vibrant vegetable world?

I tried to dream my way inside Stephen's frail blond head, where he had memorised existence. 'Most of us have gifts we never use, you know,' he said as we lay holding hands.

Stephen Porter remains one of the kindest, most thoughtful men I have ever met. I tried very hard to fall in love with him but I could not.

Lying on the bed holding hands with Stephen Porter I tried to feel what it must be like being him, not being able to see my own body, and how strange it was, since the outline of my body had come to represent the outline of myself. Lying with my eyes closed, the world dark, it seemed to me that my consciousness was situated within my physical self. How could a blind girl have had the courage to traverse the world by ship? Without being able to open my eyes and see where I was in space, where I began and ended, I felt as if I did not exist.

My eyes sprang open as the darkness pressed upon me.

'You think it's like being dead,' Stephen said. I looked at him. He was lying on his back, staring at the ceiling, speaking softly. 'What happens is that after a while all your other senses become more acute. Hearing. Smell. Touch. I don't have to look into someone's face to know what they are feeling; I just have to hear their voice.'

I did not speak.

'I'm not talking in metaphors, mate,' he said.

My blind lover went away to teach. The Department of Education sent him to Orange, the town where Super Nan grew up and where Nana Elsie was born. I visited him twice. He taught farm boys and girls who did not care if French was the language of romance. He lived in a little flat above the main street and together we walked out of the town and along roads that cut through brown open land scattered with sheep.

We never decided not to see each other, or even spoke of it. I did not know how to be intimate except through my body, as if I believed that in opening the door of my lips or my sex I had opened the door to myself.

We let each other drift away, Stephen Porter and me, him with his metaphorical eyes that had memorised the world.

FIFTY-THREE

The boss lover

BEFORE LONG SHE IS PREGNANT.

She knows she is pregnant because her girlish pink nipples take on a rich dark hue and a strange brown line runs down her belly like a tattoo. The smell of eggs revolts her.

How did she get pregnant when like every girl in the whole world she is on the pill?

And who is the father?

The shadow lover?

Stephen Porter?

Surely not Leonardo della Francesca?

Ro accompanies her to the abortion clinic where the Suspicious Wanderer disgraces herself by sobbing as the act is performed by a kindly Chinese doctor wearing a wedding ring.

'It's all right, sweetie,' coos Ro into her ear. The kindly Chinese doctor has let Ro stand in for all the absent fathers.

Afterwards, Ro buys her an extra-large slice of carrot cake with sticky cream-cheese icing from The Pudding Shop in Glebe. Ro keeps stroking her small hand as the Suspicious Wanderer continues to cry.

'I'm such a fuckwit,' she says through her sobs.

'I know you are,' says Ro. 'Never mind.'

She is not supposed to have penetrative sex for two weeks after the abortion.

She is supposed to have the wit to say no to the plump man who wants to fuck her.

She is a feminist, a new type of woman, strong and independent, who will not birth eleven children and be at the mercy of a big fellow with a gun who cuts off her hair.

Then why is she letting the plump man into her post-abortion bed? He is not even her type, being too large, too loud, too *there*. He is a big-shot publisher, often in the news, and her occasional boss.

He says, 'Oh, come on, Debbie, these things are just arbitrary dates. I promise I'll be gentle.'

And he is. He is gentle, certainly, but she is not engaged, let alone aroused, and would in fact prefer it if he were not there. She would prefer it if she could learn to say the word 'no' instead of worrying about hurting a man's feelings or whether a man will cease to like her if she says it or refuse to give her another job. Oh, poor Suspicious Wanderer, so nice to all men!

·

That afternoon in the small bedroom in Balmain the light was blue. The curtains were cream and blew softly in the wind. There was a cry, far off, almost out of earshot. There was a man in my bed and I did not know how he got there.

FIFTY-FOUR

History

EXCEPT FOR RARE AND EXTRAORDINARY occasions, no-one knows if they are experiencing history's beginning or its end, if they have just lived through that critical moment when a seemingly inconsequential action tilts everything in an unheard-of direction. It is a well-known fact that private obstinacies take precedence over history.

Super Nan did not know when she kissed her husband goodbye that a stranger would return wishing to cut off her hair. She did not know she was living through the Great War. She was looking the other way, tying her shoelaces, and did not know what was approaching.

Super Nan did not know that she was living in the last days of the old world, when great ships still sailed the earth taking people away from their homelands forever. Her blind mother came from the village of Ahascragh, near Galway. She carried in her suitcase six goblets of the finest crystal, given to her mother by the wealthy Anglo-Irish family for whom she had worked, and which her late mother had bequeathed to her. Super Nan told me that during the journey from Ireland to Australia her mother grew watercress on a flannel so that she might have something fresh to eat. It took four months to make the crossing, and days before that to make the journey to Limerick from the house where she was born at 10 Church Avenue, Ahascragh. The house had a lemon tree in the back garden which Super Nan's mother had outlined with her fingers, inch by inch.

Super Nan saw the introduction of electricity, telephones and flushing toilets. She was there for the invention of aeroplanes and cars. In her allotted thousand months she birthed eleven children because she knew no alternative. When she was born the Wright brothers were pondering the mechanics of human flight. When she died women were on the pill and men were on the moon.

When Super Nan was a girl her Irish father, Joseph, told her stories about the bushranger Frank Gardiner, who long before had held up his carriage on the road to Orange. 'I says to him, "It's a poor house here," and Mr Gardiner dipped his hat and let us on our way,' her father said. He added that he was surprised to learn that the same man had later held up the gold escort. 'He did not appear the type,' her father said.

In 1891, the girl who would grow up into Super Nan did not know there were no more bushrangers. All she understood were her own personal obstinacies, which included a fear of bushrangers.

'Anyway, I was too scared to go to the dunny at night by myself,' she said. 'I used to get my sisters to come.'

Maud, Aggie, Josephine, Mary and Ethel standing in a line, giggling, while their scaredy-cat youngest sister, Lil, tried to pee. She was terrified a bushranger would jump out on the way to the dunny and get her.

Aggie regularly snuck around the back of the dunny and whacked it with a large stick. Lil never failed to shoot out, her pants around her ankles, running for her life.

'You'd think I'd learn, wouldn't you?' said Super Nan, giggling along with her giggling sisters, now ghosts.

Nana Elsie, Super Nan's beautiful daughter who would grow up to become my grandmother, did not know she was witnessing the birth of the atomic age. On the morning of 6 August 1945, when the bomb was dropped on Hiroshima, she was a young woman arguing with her husband, Arthur, about his long-standing refusal to learn to dance. Art worked on the docks, a reserved occupation, and, anyway, he was a bit too old to be called up. He hated dancing.

Elsie and Arthur had been to a dance the night before and Elsie had danced with a handsome captain. That morning, as she cooked Art's eggs, their argument continued. Art glowered at her and Elsie said, 'What am I supposed to do if you won't dance with me? Sit on my hands?'

At that moment, a few thousand miles to the north, husbands and wives were going up in smoke.

·

In November 1956 my mother did not know that the Cold War had just been invented. When she failed to reach selection for the Australian swimming team for the 1956 Melbourne Olympic Games she sat home and sulked. There was something going on in the Suez Canal, a place she had never heard of and could not pinpoint on a map, and the USSR had invaded Hungary.

What relevance had this to her, June Gilmore—a champion swimmer relegated again to second place? June knew she was a better all-round swimmer than Dawn Fraser, yet here she was, forced to spend weeks and weeks listening to everyone going on about Dawn's ruddy gold medals.

In the last weeks of 1956 June spent as much time as she could in her bedroom, imagining the moment when everyone would recognise the magnitude of their mistake.

As for me, I did not know that I was living in the dying days of the sexual revolution. I did not know I was experiencing those last reckless days before once again sex could kill you.

I lived in the last days of typewriters, hot metal presses, the Berlin Wall and the Union of Soviet Socialist Republics.

I was there for the invention of computers, mobile phones and the internet. I was there for the invention of time travel, when anyone could fly in a jet from one side of the world to the other, sometimes arriving the same day they had left. The rich, the poor, the Irish, the Australians and the French: anyone with a passport and enough money could go.

Throughout, my knowledge of history was suspect. Like everyone, my sensibility was personal and I experienced history from the feet up. I was full of private obstinacies, history's bit player, always looking the wrong way. You'd think I'd learn, wouldn't you?

Nonetheless, here is the world, ceaseless.

Here is the world, going on.

Where is the sound of wicked Aggie whacking her stick against the dunny wall?

Where is that lost line of giggling sisters, each with a headful of memories?

Where is the scent of the lemon tree, once traced by vanished fingers, inch by inch?

A thousand months!

Mademoiselle Emilie Joubert, let me acknowledge your longing for the smell of baking bread and the lost sound of your father's whistle before I forget.

FIFTY-FIVE

The dissolute lover

THE SKIN REMEMBERS THE SMALL triangular scar high on the left hip, made upon it when the woman was twenty-four years old, a burn mark from ironing while naked.

She was ironing naked because she was twenty-four years old and she hardly ever got dressed, being newly in the grip of a passion for that dissolute lover.

At last she left the shadow lover. At last, after five blind years, she left that lover she could not see and who was possibly a figment of her imagination. At last she went to live with that dissolute lover. Out of the frying pan and into the fire!

She left the shadow lover and all the lovers lined in a row for the dissolute lover whose skin felt like home, whose body was an answered prayer, who felt like her own physical self in male form. *Skin of my skin, breath of my breath, if I were a man I'd be you.* She wrote these words on a scrap of paper and left it by the pillow one morning as he slept. But by the time she got out of the shower she thought better of it and screwed it up.

By then the Suspicious Wanderer knew her romantic streak was fatal. By then, even though she was composed of private obstinacies, she knew enough to keep them covered up.

The dissolute older lover was a Labor Party apparatchik whose louche behaviour would eventually cause him to fall into disgrace. He had bloodshot blue eyes starting to go to seed and his wrecked, handsome face was already on the cusp of dissolving.

Her new lover was not a shadow. He was knuckle, muscle, hair, the drip of sweat, the slick pink flesh of cheek inside an open mouth. His skin was always warm and gave off a sweet fragrance, like the skin of a baby. He had full, fleshy lips like her own. He loved her mouth, her porn-star lips, which he said always looked ready, open. Her lips seemed to have found their fellows and sometimes she lay with her new lover on their shared pillow for long, unbroken minutes, kissing with their kindred lips. Like her, he loved kissing.

She lived with her new lover inside an erotic swoon, sometimes forgetting to move the car forward when the traffic lights turned green because she was remembering a particular moment from the night before. She left saucepans too long on the stove, lost her concentration while ironing, and understood what it must be like to be a teenage boy with a permanent erection. Unlike the lover who fell in love with desire, unlike the shadow lover and all those other lovers in thrall to that brief joyous throb, to that most mysterious of human seconds upon which marriages, careers, religions and kingdoms rise and fall, the dissolute lover wanted to spend his whole life in those seconds.

She had never met anyone like him.

He was irresponsible. He was a madman. He was intoxicating.

He got drunk and swallowed, smoked or snorted any drug going.

'What on earth do you see in that arsehole?' asked Ro's boyfriend, Mick, after meeting him for the first time.

The Suspicious Wanderer could not have explained that once she had seen her new lover address a rally for Aboriginal land rights. He was eloquent, electric, sexy, and secretly, guiltily, she thought it was like being at a rock concert.

Remember Justine Gervais? Even the Suspicious Wanderer detected a pattern, a penchant for men and women with a political cause and a desire to burn at the stake.

The dissolute lover described himself, smiling, as a 'sectarian leftist' and she guessed that this was intended as a joke. She did not know what it meant but laughed anyway.

'Most of them think I'm a Trotskyite mole,' he said.

Before the Suspicious Wanderer moved in with him, he woke Mick and Ro at three o'clock in the morning by turning up drunk with a vase of expensive orchids he had confiscated from the rich and which he intended to present to her. When he discovered that she wasn't home he kicked a hole in the front gate. The neighbours called the police.

·

The first time the Suspicious Wanderer slept with the dissolute lover he placed a tab of acid on her tongue. Afterwards they drove Claudette for miles, right up to Palm Beach, throwing money out the window.

They were looking for a precipice they could drive Claudette over. They shared a glorious dream of flying through the miraculous air, their hair streaming. For some reason, there were no precipices to be found. By the time they realised this, dawn was breaking and they were coming down.

They drove, laughing, all the way back to Balmain, looking out the window for the fistful of notes they had tossed to the wind.

She wished to be forgetful and reckless, like him.

After the Suspicious Wanderer moved in with the dissolute lover she took to going to work without wearing underwear, so that she could feel the pleasure of the soft wet mound between her legs. Between her legs was a sweet sticky feast, his and hers, the succulent spill of them. When she awoke in the mornings the mound of her pudenda was swollen, ripe, smeared with fragrant, gliding come so that her fingers, which loved her, naturally found their way there.

Every morning her fingers slipped in and around the delicious wet slopes of flesh, the raised blood-swelled tip, and she imagined being fucked again, him once more raising her into the air. He entered her so perfectly, so precisely, she was filled. She imagined him coming over her breasts, her face; making her watch while he fucked someone else. She imagined herself tied to a chair, her legs wide open, wanting him to fuck her instead of the other girl. Lying next to her lover in the bed, the woman tried to be quiet but once an involuntary cry escaped her lips and woke him.

'You bad girl,' he said. 'You very bad girl.' He rolled the woman onto her front and thrust into her straight away while the first orgasm was still in her.

She attracted men's stares in a way she never had before. Like a bitch in heat the woman must have emitted some secret odour. Standing at bus stops men pressed into her hand scraps of paper scrawled with their telephone numbers. Once, when she and her lover were having dinner and her lover excused himself to go to the bathroom, the restaurant manager walked quickly to their table and asked her out. Beneath her skirt the new burn high on her hip was raw and weeping.

The mark of it can be found there still.

FIFTY-SIX

The impotent lover

MEMORY IS NOT DEMOCRATIC. IT creates its own hierarchy concerning what will be at the top and what will be at the bottom. Memory decides what it remembers and what it forgets, and what emerges from the daguerreotype.

Look! The impotent lover approaches, that loyal, sweet lover who preferred sleep's caress. I knew him in the dying days of the dissolute lover, back before the birth of my son, back in those days of warm sleep.

When romance died between the dissolute lover and me, exactly two years, six months and twenty-five days into our relationship, neither of us could bear it.

When we awoke in our warm bed to discover that the erotic dream in which we had dwelt had disappeared, neither of us could stand to live instead an ordinary, companionable existence. Rather than be pitched into routine sex and routine days we sought new bodies to conquer.

In our last days together the dissolute lover returned to that which gave him succour, that is, the bodies of women. Despite his ruined face he still had about him a wrecked grace, a plaintive charm that saw the most unexpected women succumb.

I returned, too, to that which gave me succour, the bodies of men. In this we were childishly alike: we sought the restoration of ourselves through the conjuring of desire in new bodies. We believed this moved us far from the helplessness of sadness.

We hardly talked.

I recall only a few words the dissolute lover ever said to me. I recall him, drunk, making a distasteful joke at my cousin's wedding. I remember the sound he made when he came.

I remember that he once declared, 'I may be in love but I can still feel the wall behind me against my back.'

Once, in our desperate last days, I had to go to Melbourne for an editing job. In truth my mission was to talk a children's book writer down from the ledge (it is a well-known fact that the authors of children's books are the most delicate of creatures). The dissolute lover supposed me to have a rendezvous with a man I knew, a former lover, who worked for the same Melbourne publisher. By chance this former lover happened to call two days before I was due to fly out. After I hung up the phone and told the dissolute lover who it was, I saw fear upon his face.

'He's going to be in Adelaide,' I said. 'Otherwise we could have had lunch.'

Did the dissolute lover nod? He obviously believed he had overheard a coded plan for me and my former lover to meet up.

When I returned to our shared house in Sydney there was a lipstick not my own in the bathroom cabinet and red welts from fingernails not my own on the dissolute lover's warm back.

He was very insecure, despite being a Labor Party apparatchik, despite being a sectarian leftist and a celebrated madman. Critical theory is all well and good, except when life rushes in with its insistent hot breath.

In search of solace in those desperate last days, I suggested a drink to a pleasant man I occasionally worked with.

Damien was a short, dark-haired Englishman, head of the poetry department. He had tanned, swarthy skin, and did not look like my concept of an Englishman.

'That's because I've got gypsy blood,' he said, smiling, as he handed me a drink.

'Sure,' I said. 'So do I.'

'No, I have. Really. My mother is Romany.'

I was not entirely sure what a Romany was, so he proceeded to give me a short, romantic history. Before long I pictured myself travelling with him on a gaily painted narrow boat down an English canal, my feet bare, a pot of red geraniums by the door.

He said he had to go home.

He said his wife, Lorraine, would have dinner waiting. I had met her once, a pretty, fair-haired woman, a primary school teacher. I had seen photographs of their two daughters, one pretty, fair-haired like the mother, one pretty, dark-skinned like him.

He said he had to go home and then I kissed him, that magic kiss of which everyone is capable but which only some of us choose to culpably employ.

We went to a swish hotel up the road. I stood to one side while he chivalrously handed over his credit card. I had already offered mine, being a member of that new breed of women who had money and credit cards and the right to sleep with whomever we wanted.

Going up in the elevator he grew visibly more nervous. As soon as we got in the door, he raced over to the mini-bar and popped open a bottle of champagne.

'I think I've had enough,' I said. 'I'm going to run a bath. Want to join me?' I put out my cigarette.

He quickly drank from his glass then moved towards me. 'Are you sure you won't have some?'

I took the glass from him, putting it down on a table, where it made a satisfying sound. 'Come here,' I said.

We began to kiss, urgently, deeply, and I could feel the swell of him against me. His hands moved to my shirt, unbuttoning it, pulling it from my shoulders, and my hands moved to the buckle of his belt.

Soon we were entwined naked on the bed. His penis was small, hard, insistent against my thigh, a dewdrop of come glistening at its peak. We kissed and kissed, he squeezed my nipples, navigated the circumference of my breasts. I felt his hardness deflate, felt all his desire evaporate.

'I can't,' he said. 'I'm sorry.'

'Shhh,' I said. 'Never mind.'

'It's not you,' he said. 'You're beautiful. I can't believe I'm lying here beside you. I want to make love to you so much.'

'We don't have to do anything, you know,' I said. 'We can just lie here. Maybe he'll perk up.' I gave his penis a jolly little shake before chastely kissing him on the nose.

For the next two hours my gypsy colleague slept in my arms, so heavily and so deeply that my left arm began to hurt. Without waking him, I gently extracted my arm from beneath his sleeping head, gathered up my clothes, dressed, and snuck out the door.

I still admire my gypsy colleague's fidelity to love and sleep, woven from the same cloth, stitched together by our submerged dreams.

FIFTY-SEVEN

Nana Elsie, *encore—épater le bourgeois!*

ALL THROUGH THOSE DAYS, THOSE days of a hundred lovers, of my willing abasement at the hands of the shadow lover and at the feet of the dissolute lover, my refuge was Nana Elsie, whom I still loved best of all.

She knew I liked croissants, though she had never eaten one herself. If she knew I was coming to stay the night, she made a special trip from Abbotsford to Five Dock on the bus to pick up a couple from the wog shop that made them. Back then, the inner cities of the world were not gentrified. Back then, no-one but wogs had heard of a macchiato.

Nana Elsie kept a couple of tins of sweet corn kernels, too, because as a child I had liked them. My grandfather, Art, was always around, fixing up a stuck door or in the front yard, mowing or washing the car. He was an unskilled factory worker, good with his hands. Despite the fact that he could not dance, she loved him all her life, dancing or not.

·

Nana Elsie thought I could do anything. 'You've got the world at your feet,' she often said. Whenever she spoke of me it was 'Our Debbie has done this' or 'Our Debbie has done that.' I never once heard my father or mother speak about me in that way.

I never knew why Nana Elsie was so proud of me either, since I had never done anything of which to be proud. In fact, I increasingly regarded myself as a disappointing sort of person, even as someone who had done much of which to be ashamed. But always, when I was with my nan, her love turned me innocent and singled me out, absolving me from blame.

She seemed proud of the fact that I existed.

She seemed to be the only person in the whole world who was.

Nana Elsie never said a harsh word about my poor choice of lovers, not even when I chanced upon the dissolute lover, drunk at my cousin's wedding, asking for her opinion about my work as a part-time prostitute.

Does that even qualify as a joke? I suppose it had something to do with *épater le bourgeois*, with the same *eat the rich* sentiment then popular with the sectarian left. The fact that Nana Elsie was neither rich nor a member of the bourgeois was irrelevant. What the dissolute lover intended, I think, was to set the cat among the pigeons of marriage and monogamy, and to make clear the ringing fact that he was trying to break free from the template of ordinary existence.

I confess that I gained a certain satisfaction from setting a rabid dissolute lover upon my family, though I never intended to set him upon Nana Elsie.

'He's taken a drop too much,' Nana Elsie said later, which was as far as her loyal lips would take her.

At the same wedding my father threatened to beat up the dissolute lover, over what I do not know. I was on the dance floor when I saw them standing up, scuffling drunkenly across the table. My tipsy mother was already manoeuvring my father away.

I should have known the dissolute lover would make a pass at my sister at the same wedding. She would have responded, too, except that at the time she happened to be with a jealous, possessive millionaire named Carl. Carl the millionaire wanted to beat up the dissolute lover as well, so we left the wedding reception before the dissolute lover had the chance to secure Jane's telephone number and before he had any further opportunities to *épater le bourgeois*.

Nana Elsie said to me afterwards, 'There's nothing like family, Debbie. Friends are all very well, but it's family who stand by you when the chips are down.'

She would never have acknowledged that families are frequently the reason that the chips are down.

FIFTY-EIGHT

My son

JUST BEFORE MY MOTHER DIED, when she no longer wore turbans and had forgotten everything but for her tongue, which had not yet forgotten desire, the staff at the nursing home where she lived gave her a doll. It was a great ugly thing, a cloth body stuffed with wool, with plastic arms and legs sewn on. Its head was plastic too, with a face no baby had ever possessed, and in its plastic scalp was woven real golden hair.

As soon as she was given the doll, my mother's arms rose into that ancient female crook to cradle her baby. Somewhere inside that memoryless woman was an unbroken bodily memory of caring. My mother, my lover! Would that you could once again scratch my back with your red-painted fingernails!

In those first suckling months with my own baby son we dreamt and slept, awoke and dreamt again.

My body fell in love with his and his with mine. I was never more clearly the sum of my parts than in those first milky days.

FIFTY-NINE

The romantic lover

SUPER NAN'S MOTHER, ROSE, SAILED to the other side of the world even though she was blind.

Super Nan loved to tell the story of how her parents met, how her father, Joseph, passed Rose in the street and fell in love with her on the spot. He could see that she was blind, and yet she looked straight into his eyes. This was years before they met each other in Australia. This was in Ireland, long before Joseph became the owner of the finest hotel in Orange.

Joseph, from Limerick, fell in love with Rose, from Ahascragh, near Galway, because of her penetrating blind eyes.

'It's true,' Super Nan said. 'Some people fall in love the minute they see someone and love them till the day they die.'

Is it any wonder I was a romantic?

'Anyway,' said Super Nan, 'the strange thing was that although Mother was what you would call legally blind, whenever anybody spoke to her she always turned her head towards them and looked straight into their eyes. People don't expect blind people to look at them. Or at least they expect them to turn their heads clumsily towards the speaker, to look at their forehead or their ears or their nose. They don't expect a blind person to look straight at them.'

Wanting to find out why Rose's beautiful cloudy-blue blind eyes looked so penetratingly into his own, Joseph followed her down a Galway street, into a shop and into his future. He was on an errand for his father, a poor farmer, who had sent his son all the way from Limerick to Galway to obtain the carriage promised to him free by the wealthy uncle of a neighbour. Joseph had never been to Galway and was lost.

Following Rose into the shop, Joseph learnt that a blind girl is a bible, a dictionary, a book of common prayer, that a blind girl is a memory box. She had memorised the world, the shape of its streets, the words of its songs and the number of steps to the grocery shop. She remembered the entire six verses of every hymn in church each Sunday and knew the number of steps in the paving stones in the path leading to the lemon tree in the back garden.

Joseph followed her round and round. Finally, she turned and looked him in the eye. 'Will you please stop following me?' she said in a surprisingly loud voice.

Straight away Joseph left the shop.

He stood outside, waiting for her to emerge. He did not know what he was going to say to her, or indeed if she would answer him if he did. As he waited for the blind girl, nervously twisting his best handkerchief in his fingers, the brother of his neighbour from Limerick happened to pass. 'Morning, Joseph,' he said, tipping his hat. 'What brings you to these parts?'

By the time Joseph had explained his mission, the brother of his neighbour was dragging him away to his uncle. 'What a very good piece of luck this is, Joseph!' he said. 'You being lost and me finding you!'

Joseph turned back towards the shop only to glimpse the blind girl emerge, a basket over her arm, and hurry away.

He did not set eyes on her again till four years later, in Australia, on the other side of the earth, when she applied for a job as a scullery maid at the house where he was working.

Super Nan said her father had the Irish way with words. He spoke of Rose as keeping 'the world in her head' and said that it wasn't long before he wished to be kept there too.

'He was a bit of a poet, was Father,' Super Nan said proudly. 'He could charm the birds from the trees if he had a mind to.'

But Super Nan's favourite part of the romantic story of her mother and father was not their meeting. It was the part her father told again and again, the part when Joseph asked Rose what she would choose to look at if by some miracle she was allowed to see for one day.

Rose turned her face towards him, looked with accuracy into his eyes, and replied, 'I would look at you, Joseph. I would look at you.'

SIXTY

The bottom lover

I HAVE SOMETIMES IDLY WONDERED if Joseph's desiring tongue ever sought Rose's bottom. Did anyone even have a bottom in those days?

I have a bottom, not large-buttocked and rolling, there-she-blows, like my darling Ro. A small bottom, mine, jaunty.

A bottom nonetheless sought by numerous tongues and lips, including those of the lover whose lips were long and wide, what I thought of as Scandinavian lips, a generous opening too large for his face.

He was blond, the lover with Scandinavian lips, with big, even white teeth which suited his mouth. When he kissed, the kiss spread across your face, from your lips to your cheeks to your hair.

I slept with him four times.

It is not my mouth that remembers.

He was an Australian actor who later became famous, so that if I tell you his name you will know it. These days he is seen only with beautiful actresses but every time I chance upon a picture of him and a famous actress in a celebrity magazine I wonder which part of her body his mouth seeks.

All he ever wanted from me was my bottom: for me to turn and raise my jaunty arse to his mouth.

At first I thought it was an act of bravado, that he might be the kind of man who performs cunnilingus on the first night, never to show his face there again. At first I thought his rolling me over and the migration of his tongue to that most private puckered place was a continuation of this bravado, a first-time performance designed to impress.

As it happens, I am oddly squeamish about my bottom, preferring it to go about its business with the minimum of attention. As it happens, when his tongue began to probe that most intimate of orifices, my body went into a kind of inner clench.

I began to worry about whether I had cleaned myself thoroughly (despite the fact that we had just shared a bath) or indeed whether one could ever clean a bottom sufficiently.

But the man with the Scandinavian lips could not get enough. His tongue felt hard and pointed and I imagined it to be forked like a snake's, so particularly and deftly did it dart in and out, around and around. I was wondering when he would stop, and whether this was a prelude to sodomy, which I happen not to enjoy.

He went on and on, groaning with pleasure, while my fingers gripped the sheets.

At last his mouth slowly journeyed upwards, to my buttocks, to my back. When he reached the curve of my neck, he rolled me over again and began to kiss my face. I could smell myself, a faintly cloying, sweet smell, and when he reached my lips there was no mistaking the whiff of shit.

By now he was inside me, crazed with desire, and I turned my head from side to side in what he might have supposed was frenzied lust but which was in fact a bid to evade his soiled mouth.

When he came, he cried out. He collapsed on top of me and lay panting, still holding me fiercely. 'Oh God,' he said. 'You have no idea how magnificent that was.'

I slept with him four times, and every single time he sought my bottom.

'Weirdo,' said Ro.

'Perv,' said Steph.

I sometimes wondered if Ro and Steph knew more about me than any lover, lost or found, could ever know.

I was almost thirty, in transit, a property of the people even though I secretly considered bottoms to be privately owned.

SIXTY-ONE

The deflowerer, again

THE SUSPICIOUS WANDERER SOON ARRIVES at that wistful, elegiac place where she begins to look back with longing.

Because her experience of having the first flower picked from her body was a joyful one, over the years the memory of it had grown more and more beautiful. She is starting to look back with a sigh.

One bright summer morning she chances upon her deflowerer, Jonathan Jamieson, in the street. Instantly the wretchedness dogging her falls away, the sorrow rooted in her since the dying days of the dissolute lover, since her abandonment of that lover oblivion, since the day when she sobbed for the absent fathers and discovered in her bed a lover she did not like or even care to know. Has Jonathan Jamieson come to save her?

Her deflowerer is to be married the following month. He is deeply in love with his wife-to-be, but he says that he has never stopped loving the Suspicious Wanderer.

It is ten years since they lay together.

They make love, weep, and the Suspicious Wanderer begs his forgiveness. All the sorrows of love, its pity and its failures, gather round.

'You were so kind!' she says. 'I'm so, so sorry!'

He holds her weeping head against his chest for a long time, stroking her hair. She smells again the smell of his caramel skin, feels again the feel of his steady hands, and notes how gently he holds her.

Oh! What is wrong with her that she should have walked away from his steady hands and his eyes with their heavy, dark lashes?

'I can't see you again, you know,' he says.

'I know.'

After he has gone she makes a vow that, like him, she will strive to find someone to love.

She is almost thirty. She fears that her character is already set, fixed until death. She fears that she is destined to live out her life within the poor confines of her unwitting compulsions.

SIXTY-TWO

Super Nan

BUT WHERE IN THE WORLD does the Suspicious Wanderer belong? Is it in Sydney, Australia, or Paris, France?

And—most troubling of all—to whom does she belong? Does nobody claim her but her nan?

She feels she has lived all her days in voluntary blindness. She feels as if she is approaching some hidden, decisive moment. She might have given herself away too freely, too easily, in a way that reveals how little she loves her body as her own. She lost her body so long ago she has forgotten that she lost it.

Once again the Suspicious Wanderer flees the scene, from one side of the world to the other. Unlike her great-grandmother Lil, who was once frightened of bushrangers, and unlike her blind great-great-grandmother Rose, who grew watercress upon a flannel, she can time travel. But, like them and like Mademoiselle Emilie Joubert and like that perished line of giggling sisters, she belongs to the unbroken river and to the current's remorseless flow.

Two days before she leaves again for Paris, the woman goes with Nana Elsie to visit Super Nan in the nursing home. Super Nan looks tiny in the bed.

'Hello, Mum,' says Nana Elsie, 'we've brought you some mango.'

Super Nan is ninety-nine years old. In three days she turns a hundred. A hundred! That small head full of years. Her eyes are the size of currants, plonked down on either side of her nose, which appears to have grown. The girl who was once famous for being the most beautiful girl in Orange has a nose so large it resembles one of those fake noses held on with a piece of elastic.

'Come here, love,' she says.

The Suspicious Wanderer gives her a kiss. 'Hello, Super Nan.'

She has lost her wits. Before she moved into the nursing home from Nana Elsie's house in Five Dock, she was rising at three o'clock in the morning to cook a baked dinner, which often involved trying to cook the cat.

'How did you get in?' Super Nan says.

'We just walked in,' the Suspicious Wanderer replies.

Super Nan looks at her daughter. 'Who's she?'

'That's Elsie,' the Suspicious Wanderer says. 'Your daughter. Your favourite girl.'

Super Nan looks at Nana Elsie as she goes about the business of pulling up a chair by the bed, opening the Tupperware container of freshly sliced mango, and finding a clean spoon.

'Come on, Mum,' Nana Elsie says. 'Open up.'

·

Sometimes the Suspicious Wanderer comes by herself to the nursing home. After she has visited Super Nan she always goes to the sitting room, where there are other old people whom nobody comes to visit. Survivors of themselves, washed up on some far shore, they are immeasurably happy if she sits with them, taking their bony hands between her fleshy fingers.

She particularly likes one old man with a thick Scottish accent.

'What are those people doing?' he asks her once, indicating the other old people in the room.

'I don't know,' she says.

One of the cheery nursing assistants tells the Suspicious Wanderer that the old man is originally from Edinburgh, and that he came to Australia as a young man to teach. His wife is long dead; they had no children.

The next time the Suspicious Wanderer goes to the nursing home she takes with her a framed photograph of Edinburgh that she saw for sale in an op shop for fifty cents.

But the old man is not in the sitting room.

'He's had a stroke,' a nurse tells her. 'He's in his room, number fourteen. He can't speak.'

In his room the old man is by the window, lying in a reclining chair, covered by a rug.

'Hello,' she says. 'I hope you won't mind a visitor. Look what I found.'

She walks towards the window, holding up the photograph. He tries to turn his poor, twisted head. His face has fallen in, one side completely collapsed; there is drool on his chin.

He makes a gurgling sound.

He looks at the photograph.

The last time the Suspicious Wanderer saw her great-grandmother, Super Nan asked her what Paris was like.

'Is it as good as Sydney?' she said.

She really did ask that. The Suspicious Wanderer wrote it down on a piece of paper because she was so struck by the clarity of the question.

She never got to tell Super Nan that Sydney or Paris, Melbourne or Boston, no-one said 'Anyway' like her.

SIXTY-THREE

The wine lover

THAT LIQUID OF THE FIVE senses, of myth and desire! Pearly, clear, tawny, the palest straw yellow, how I love your dance upon the tongue, the sound of you being poured into a glass, the smell of you.

The shimmering ice-cold wine I drank with my new husband at a table in the garden of a faded hotel in the spa town of Royat, France. The leaves were starting to fall from the chestnut trees around our heads and on the table a perfect late-summer peach and two honeymoon glasses of the most fragrant, delicious grass-coloured wine I had ever drunk in my life.

That first glass of champagne we drank after the birth of our son, the cork hitting the ceiling, the champagne overflowing from the bottle, spilling onto my husband's shaking hands. The bubbles swarming in my throat, fizzing, bursting, excitement made manifest.

·

The juicy Corsican wine I drank at Horatia's stone house, that object lover with whom I was in love. We were on its roof, seated at the long wooden dining table under the stars, eating silvery fish. The fish might have swum up from the sea through the valley to our table, so fresh and alive did they seem.

I turned my face to heaven, the wash of wine in my mouth, intoxicated by the air, the stars, by the stones beneath my feet warm from the sun. I had no money, no savings, no house of my own and yet I felt myself to be richer than Croesus.

The mysterious alchemy of the grape turning to wine, the rows and rows of vines near Fitou in the south of France turning orange, red, russet, burnt, in the days before the *vendange*. Farmers, princes, the rich, the poor, everyone is equal before the grape, the workers filling up their plastic petrol containers with *vin de pays* through a rubber hose, the titled rich strolling through private vineyards as manicured as the finest tended gardens. The mysterious alchemy of the sugar-filled fruit turns everyone *égalé* because hierarchies disappear before it.

The mysterious alchemy, too, of getting drunk, the wine working its way within me, running in my veins like a fresh, cool river, loosening my limbs, my shyness, my cares. The way being drunk makes me feel happy, loved and loving, everything wrong miraculously put right. The stars are reachable, the world has a meaning, and if alcohol is a depressant its message is undeliverable while wine runs like a stimulant in my veins, rendering anything possible. I know boys who have leapt off bridges and girls who have run naked down the street while that fresh, cool river runs exhilaratingly fast over fears, worries, over every rock blocking the way.

That happy memory of drinking wine from one of the remaining fine crystal goblets carried in the suitcase of a sixteen-year-old blind girl from Ahascragh.

Drinking wine from such an object was like supping with memory itself, raising a glass in the company of ghosts. I never once raised one of those goblets without being conscious of my pulsing fingers against the stem. I felt my fingers to be alive, sensate, warm, as the fingers of that blind girl, Rose, had been too. I felt the tracery of her fingers against my own and the imprint of her lips as I sipped. Each of us, every one, joined in the democracy of our transit.

Drinking wine from those glasses turned every wine aromatic to the tongue, too. There was something about the shape of the fine glass, the sensory feel of it against the fingers, the way the bowl of the crystal sat upon the stem that distilled every wine to its essence.

The glasses fitted my hands perfectly, as if especially made for them.

Each glass had a fine turned rim at the top, perfectly shaped for swallowing lips. Just below the little rim, the glass was etched with a curly delicate pattern, so that the full fat centre of each glass sparkled in the light.

Now there is one sparkling goblet remaining.

SIXTY-FOUR

Paris

IN PARIS THE WOMAN, WHO was almost thirty, with no house or money or children, stayed in one of Horatia's large spare rooms in her apartment on the rue Saint-Jacques.

The apartment was enormous by Parisian standards, and opened up to the sky on both sides, with floor-to-ceiling windows. On one side it overlooked the busy street, but the windows were double-glazed and when they were closed every room was silent. On the other side there was a pretty square belonging to the Sorbonne, with trees and moss-covered statues.

Rue Saint-Jacques was once the starting point for pilgrims leaving Paris for Santiago de Compostela.

'You are reversing direction,' said Horatia, whose opinion of Australia was low. She assumed that every young Australian woman would naturally wish to join the pilgrimage to Paris. 'What does your country offer except sun?'

The woman felt a hot surge of emotion. 'Everything!' she said.

'Everything for the body,' said Horatia. 'If you wish a sort of vegetable happiness I am sure Australia would be most suitable. It is the same with America.'

The woman hated it when Horatia, who had never been to America or Australia, made such pronouncements. 'You're being unfair, Horatia,' she said.

'Being unfair is one of life's great pleasures,' Horatia replied. 'When you are as old as me you may be as unfair as you like.' She smiled and offered the woman another kir royal and a rose-coloured macaroon.

During the day the woman walked the streets, looking for she knew not what. She was wondering if she had fallen for some old idea of Paris that was no longer true, if it ever had been.

What she noted with her fallible eye was the beauty of her object lover, the Pont Marie, still barnacled with vanished wishes.

Everywhere she saw the marriage of stone, window, light, air, the convergence of separate elements which together fashioned Paris's architectural splendour.

Horatia had a theory that people instinctively preferred civilised Paris and its desire to call beauty to heel or else barbarous Rome and its desire to let beauty go.

'You can tell a lot about someone when you know if they prefer Paris or Rome,' Horatia said.

'Can't you like both?' the woman asked.

'Definitely not,' Horatia said.

·

Walking the streets each day the woman noted that even the poorest shopped carefully for the plumpest fruit, the sweetest peach, for the mouthful of sugar from the sun-heavy grape.

Across the street from Horatia's flat an old building was being restored and every day at lunchtime the dusty workers stopped to eat under a tree in the courtyard. They took out their napkins, their baguettes and several different kinds of cured meats and cheeses. They shared a bottle of red wine, *vin de pays*, which they drank from little plastic cups. '*Bonjour, mademoiselle*,' they said courteously as she passed.

She went by metro to Saint-Denis, formerly the stronghold of Communist Paris, part of the working-class *banlieue*, home to Arabs and Pieds-Noirs and Maghrebis. This was another Paris, but still recognisably Paris. She noted the council tower blocks and the families with too many children but she also noted the care with which veiled women chose tomatoes at the street market. Men looked too long at her and women too narrowly.

Like them, she did not have money, but unlike them, she had the luxury of being able to pause between the hours in which she earned the notes she exchanged for food and shelter. These people on the outskirts of Paris appeared to live their whole lives without pausing.

As she walked she thought about retraining as a nurse, or as a teacher, moving to a Third World country to live a more useful life, helping children construct an existence without want, to live working lives capable of incorporating pauses. What made a good life? Was it worth striving to live a life punctuated by pauses? She wondered if the quality of life might be measured in leisure hours.

The Suspicious Wanderer walked the streets of Paris from morning till dusk, looking and looking. She wasn't on holiday, she was pausing in the midst of existence, considering her next move, knowing how fortunate she was to be able to do so. She had the luxury of considering herself a recovering romantic, flushing romance from her blood, as if killing an addiction or infection.

She was also running out of what little money she had. Since there was nothing romantic about running out of money, the Suspicious Wanderer turned her mind to making some.

SIXTY-FIVE

The beach lover

HOW I LOVE LYING BACK upon the sand, spread-eagled, running hot sand through my fingers. How I love floating free and defenceless on oceans, the Pacific, the Mediterranean, the Atlantic, my body spilling out into the vast arms of the comforting, cruel sea.

I love crashing into the mighty force of waves pulled by the moon. Up! Pushing up from the floor of the sea to jump over white rushing foam or diving down just in time, my happy feet tickled by the froth.

The taste of the sea, the roar of it! Having to shout across the ferocious waves, noisier than traffic, louder than a plane taking off. *Don't go out too far!* I shouted to my son when he was twelve, thirteen, fourteen, still believing his body to be the equal of the ocean. He could never hear me over the crash and tumult of the waves, no matter how loud I shouted, no matter how I could already picture the rip which would carry him away.

·

Once my new French lover and I went to stay in Horatia's house on Corsica, that house I loved. It was late in the season, chilly by sunset, but at midday we floated on our backs in the calm warm sea. The ocean held us up and the sun stroked our faces and one day I swear I fell asleep in the arms of the sea. Either that or I entered a strange, dreamlike state, hypnotised by the gentle rock of the water holding me up. Everything in me armed and upright against the strains of life slowly unclenched, until at last I felt myself to be without edges, indistinguishable from the vast, apparently boundless sea. I floated into it, right inside it, so that there was no beginning to me, no end. I was going down, in, becoming water, salt, when I awoke with a shock, screamed, and stood up. '*Ça va?*' my new lover asked, standing up too.

'I think I was turning into a fish,' I said, and laughed.

Strangely, I was not frightened.

Oh, the thick, coarse sand of a wet beach on the Côte Sauvage in early spring, the wind snapping, whipping our hair into our faces!

The silky white sand along the coast of Queensland, miles and miles of unpeopled sand, devoid of footprints. Once I climbed an enormous sand dune on Stradbroke Island and Ro took a photograph of me naked and unbroken, the white sand all around, showing only the smallest border of blue, cloudless sky above my head.

The strange blackish sand of Sweetwater Beach near Loutro, Crete, where I once spent the days observing two old men, Athenians, who travelled there every summer. From sunrise to sunset the two friends spent the day up to their necks in the sand, periodically emerging like two giant turtles to walk slowly to the water, where they rinsed themselves before crawling back up the beach.

The glorious summer I lived with my son across the road from Rainbow Beach after I lost my husband. A broken-down fibro beach shack with lumpy, sweat-covered sofas of indeterminate fabric and a kitchen unchanged since it was built in 1950.

The local Aborigines believed the coloured sands were caused by a spirit falling into the cliffs, infusing the sand with all the colours of the rainbow.

We loved it there, my son and me, falling into bed when we grew tired, getting up when we awoke and running across the grass to the coloured sand, then throwing ourselves into the slapping ocean. We grew lean and tanned, the tips of my boy's hair growing fairer, his bare feet rough and horny. We were at home in our skins, and hardly ever wore clothes.

'Why doesn't everybody live at the beach?' he asked me.

'I'm sure I don't know, sweetheart,' I replied.

My son thought every beach had sand with the colours of a rainbow.

Once we spent the day walking at least sixteen kilometres up the beach, collecting gold, yellow, orange, pink and blue sands, so that at the end of the day we had a glass jar which held a captured rainbow.

I still have that glass jar.

It sits upon my windowsill here in my house in Fanjeaux, a slice of Australia; memory rendered visible.

Ro never loved the beach. She preferred the mountains. Her skin was fair, for she was meant for the mists and the rain of a town in Yorkshire or Pembrokeshire.

Ro did not like the sand or the heat or the wind and only accompanied me to Stradbroke Island that bright day as an act of kindness. She kept her large bottom swathed in a sarong from Bali and I told her she looked like one of Gauguin's Tahitian wives but for her pale skin, which was already sunburnt.

That burning sun! That sea! Those sands! So many of my numbered days have been spent as happy as a clam, rinsed by the water, baked by the sun, unspooled on the earth's beaches.

SIXTY-SIX

The beautiful lover

RO CAME TO PARIS TO visit me, staying in another of Horatia's spare rooms. I was giving English conversation classes, running them out of Horatia's flat, mainly to her wealthy friends and many acquaintances. Most did not have a hope of mastering a stroke of English but appeared to enjoy coming, possibly because of the English tea and exquisite macaroons accompanying the lessons. In the mornings I worked on proofreading jobs and editing work.

Ro had broken up with Mick, after many years of an on-off relationship, because she had decided she wanted a baby and Mick did not.

'Why don't you have a child by yourself if you want one?' Horatia asked.

'Do you know how hard it is to be a single mother?' Ro said. 'I've got too many friends who are single mothers to have any idealistic notions about it.'

Horatia sniffed. 'Personally I can never understand why any woman would want to have a child. It compromises one's life too much.'

'I want my life compromised,' said Ro.

'Madness,' said Horatia.

Later, Horatia took me aside and suggested I advise my friend that generally men did not like women to carry too much fat around the rear end. 'If she wants to attract a man in order to have a baby, she should start with that bottom.'

'Horatia!'

She tapped the side of her nose. 'I don't mind telling her if you won't.'

Ro was just as enamoured of Horatia as I was, and especially admired her take-no-prisoners pronouncements. 'I've never met a woman with so much gall,' she said.

'Do you think it's because she's a lesbian?' I asked. 'You know, she hasn't spent her life pussy-footing around men like we have.'

'Pussy-footing. Interesting choice of words.'

Horatia was ceaseless in her quest to persuade us to move to Paris permanently.

'I could never live here full-time,' Ro said. 'Paris is like a film set. It's not real to me.'

Horatia smiled. 'That's simply because you haven't lived here long enough. In time you'd see that it is just like anywhere else, except for the French genius of appreciating what is best in life.'

'Hmm,' said Ro. 'Tell that to the poor souls crammed into public housing. Or to the Algerian kids who can't get into French universities.'

'They all still flock to France, don't they?'

'Only because they mistakenly think they are coming to a better life,' said Ro.

'They are,' said Horatia.

'I hate how smug the French are. And you're not even French, Horatia! You must know that it was the French genius for appreciating what is best in life that caused them to surrender to the Germans. They didn't want Paris to get bombed.'

Horatia smiled again. 'That's a good enough reason to surrender, isn't it? For beauty's sake?'

I met the beautiful lover at the opening of an exhibition of sculptures by an old friend of Horatia's, a handsome Frenchwoman. I noticed him at once, and not only because he was one of the few men in the room.

I saw immediately that he was beautiful, breathtakingly so, and that his beauty stranded him in a lonely place. It had cleared a circle around him, a space no-one dared enter. He had a glass in his hand and everyone who passed glanced at him, covertly or overtly, not once but twice, three times, hardly believing what they were seeing.

He was obviously a model. In Paris I had sometimes come across others of these beautiful human specimens, who did not appear to have the same proportions as ordinary mortals. I once followed an exquisitely proportioned girl out of the metro and onto the street because I could not believe my eyes. She was flawless.

The beautiful man had finely cut bones and a full sensuous mouth that bore a curious resemblance to my father's.

'Don't,' said Ro.

'Too late,' I said as I walked towards him. 'Hello,' I said.

'How are you?' he said, turning and giving me a smile that almost knocked me off my feet.

The beautiful man turned out to be a painter, English, not yet represented by a decent gallery. Straight away he told me that his work had won no major prizes and consequently it had attracted little critical attention. He said he sold his work here and there, in Paris and in London, but that he mainly made his living as a model—a photographic model, not an artist's model. He also did catwalk shows.

'I knew it!' I cried.

'Everybody seems to guess,' he replied, a little mournfully.

I realised that I had seen his photographs in fashion magazines. He told me that he also featured in a large billboard ad for razors, which I remembered passing every time I caught the bus to Nana Elsie's. In the billboard photo he looked like a man who had never known misfortune and would never meet illness or decay. He looked like someone who would never experience death personally.

His name was Richard. He said it was kind of me to talk to him.

We swapped phone numbers. I said goodbye, in a reserved sort of way. Already I wanted to distinguish myself from all the other women who had drowned him in wishes.

I intended to wait for him to call and vowed not to call him first.

When Richard suggested meeting at a bar in the Marais, I was careful to keep a formal, respectful distance. I was keeping my dying romantic wishes well concealed beneath my longing skin.

When he suggested a drink at his flat after dinner, I said no.

'Are you saving yourself?' he asked, giving me his beautiful smile.

'Yes,' I said.

Ro and Horatia both advised caution.

'The beautiful are a race apart,' said Horatia.

'I know,' I said.

'Beauty has its own rules,' Horatia added, just in case.

Richard lived in an apartment in the Marais, in a little Jewish quarter off the rue de Rivoli.

'Bloody tourists,' he said, leading me through a throng of people to his flat for the first time.

When he walked down the street, women nudged each other and people sometimes stopped walking altogether to stare. Like a beautiful woman, his beauty defined him, and he was condemned to a life of either justifying it, or else pretending that it did not exist. He chose the latter.

His apartment doubled as a studio. His bed was a mattress on the floor, and every surface, every wall was covered with his paintings and drawings and with photographs he had cut out from magazines, from postcards, from newspapers. The effect was beautiful, a wild disarray of colour and line and form, and I spent the first hour gazing at the walls. His paintings were extraordinary.

'Even I can tell that these are very, very good,' I said.

'Thank you,' he said. 'It's nerve-racking betting everything you've got on your own talent. There's always a good chance you won't be any good.'

I wished I could bet everything I had on something worthwhile. Should I bet on him? Was he the perfect lover, here at last?

The beautiful lover did not talk much and seemed to find speech an effort. 'Words are useless for describing the world,' he said that first evening in his apartment.

I had made the fatal female mistake of asking what he was thinking. I couldn't believe I had tripped up so easily!

'I didn't ask you to describe the world,' I said. 'I only asked what you were thinking.'

'I'm thinking of soup, a sky I saw one night in Tunisia, of the lines of that stupid Morrissey song. I'm thinking of the number three and the word zero. I'm also thinking about the meaning of life.' It was possibly the longest speech I had heard from him.

'You are not,' I said.

'I might be,' he replied, smiling.

I still suffered from that female complaint of wanting to know everything. He had already told me that when he was fifteen he had saved a girl from drowning. Being literal-minded, a girl with no imagination, I imagined that this event merely prefigured every other drowning woman in his life who would cling to his neck.

When we finally lay upon his mattress later that night I wondered if the wishes of drowning girls were the reason the beautiful lover approached me in such a nervy, startled way, as if at any moment he might be dragged under.

In the act of love he was soft and fluttery, and came almost as soon as he entered me. 'Sorry, my love,' he said. 'That was like a sparrow.'

'What do you mean?'

'A sparrow's fuck,' he said. 'Fast and light.'

But every time after that was like the first: a soft, gentle flutter as of startled wings, a spurt, over in seconds. Nevertheless I enjoyed the birdlike grace of it.

He soon made it clear that he was already leaving. 'I'm moving to Tunisia in May,' he said.

'Wonderful,' I said. 'I've never been to Tunisia. I'll come and visit.'

'Yes, you must,' he said, in the same way that people often say they must catch up sometime.

He was not my boyfriend. We rarely went out together and when we did I found the experience unsettling because of the stares.

I never established the beautiful lover's exact relationship to me.
I could not tell you what I was to him either.

The last night I spent with him before he moved to Tunisia I sat
in a chair opposite the mattress on the floor, itemising the beauty
of his face.

I noted the architecture of the bones beneath his skin, the
well-cut lines of his nose and his cheekbones. I noted the place-
ment of his eyebrows over his eyes, each a perfectly sculpted arch.
I especially admired the way his lips were shaped, perfectly drawn
as if modelled on an artist's best drawing.

I left the bedside light on and lay down beside him. His eyelids
flickered in a dream, his mouth fell slightly open like the fat,
happy mouth of a satiated suckling baby. I reached out to brush
the hair from his forehead and he flinched.

I felt important, having a member of beauty's royalty asleep
beside me. I will always be grateful that human beauty once came
fleetingly to rest upon my pillow.

SIXTY-SEVEN

Breasts

A TRACERY OF FINGERS, A body mapped.

A body outlined, drawn, weighed down by the impressions of a million fingerprints, lighter than air.

The tracery of fingerprints a body has known: the comforting touch, the erotic stroke, the arm pulled too hard by a lost husband, the wrist grabbed too insistently by a skinny boy child seeking your immediate attention.

How you loved lying next to that boy, skin to skin, nose to nose. When that boy was a baby lying tucked into your arm he turned his head towards yours, so that his small face was directly in the path of your warm breath. The tiny hands of that baby boy, splayed against your breast, the miniscule fingerprints engraved with his signature.

How he loved your breasts, how he made them new again. All those years of hungry lovers sucking at the teat! All those mouths, all those lips, until his! His lips were unkissed, his breath unsullied, as pure as clouds. His new lips washed your lips clean, made your body new again. His lips washed an old heart fresh, made you a virgin.

Once, in those first milky days, you are standing under the shower when milk spurts from your breasts. You hadn't known that your nipples contain barely perceptible tiny perforations, so that when the milk comes it sprays out, as if from a shower rose.

How your breasts turned into two new living creatures upon your chest. You have never had big bosoms before, and now you look like a page-three girl.

Your new husband is pleased.

Your new husband is not pleased about the baby.

He feels the baby is taking up too much of your attention.

He feels the baby's cries are too loud.

He feels put upon, unjustly harnessed to the onerous task of bringing in the bacon.

When you hold your new husband's head against your page-three breasts it is like cradling a horse's head because the baby's head is no bigger than an orange.

Your hungry lovers loved your breasts, page three or not. A fine bosom, high, pink-nippled, girlish. The only thing that changed after the birth of your son was that the pink, girlish hue turned a deeper colour. They remained girlish and high for the longest time, long after your son stopped supping at their teats, long after he was grown, long after endless men had stopped sucking upon them, long after Steph lost a breast to cancer.

How you and Steph mourned that lost breast. Steph never had children and she told you her breasts remained sexual emblems. 'I have to look at them in an entirely new way now,' she said and then she laughed. 'Correction. I have to look at "it" in an entirely new way.' She tried to laugh but it turned into a sob.

By then our bodies were turning into maps, figurative representations of what we had lived, loved and suffered. Soon, anyone would be able to read our histories in the fault lines of our skins, in the former succulence of our lips, in the archaeology of our shameless, ruined faces. How vain we started, how humbled we finished.

SIXTY-EIGHT

The house she fell in love with

THE HOUSE, THAT OBJECT LOVER, was never hers. It belonged to Horatia, who had it designed to her specifications.

One blue evening in Paris, Horatia told her about it, but nothing Horatia said prepared her for its beauty.

The house was in Corsica. A mountain rose up behind it, looming, preposterous, too full for the eye, snow-capped, even in blazing summer. So close it seemed anyone might reach it in a hundred steps.

At the front of the house was a valley, fashioned with low hills, and here and there a great craggy string of cliffs arose, with little villages perched on top. Directly across from the house was a village the same colour as the cliffs, carved from it, a church at its peak with bells ringing out the hours.

The house was a mix of Corsican stone, left natural, and whitewashed stone, modernist, like a Frank Lloyd Wright design.

Inside were cool white tiles, some scattered with the flokati rugs Horatia had collected in Greece over the years.

The house looked like a sculpture. It consisted of several cubes linked by passages and walkways, ponds and rockeries, and each section had its own distinct and memorable character.

On top of one cube was a roof garden with three-hundred-and-sixty-degree views which looked over all the other roofs of the house and down into the valley and hills below and where she drank a glass of juicy wine and turned her face up to the stars. The mountain behind, the sea far, far away, the folds and sweeps of the valley, green, tawny, more Italian than French, with stone villages atop hills, church spires, and yellow ridges dotted with pines. Every night they ate dinner on the roof and watched the boundless sky change from blue to orange to pink to purple before melting into a deep, inky black.

In the garden around the house were fig trees, grapes, cherries, insects, birds; the air was always scented and hot and quick with life. Every afternoon she dozed in the heat, naked on a white sheet, weightless.

She wanted to live in that house forever, to feel her feet upon its cool white tiles.

She wanted to whitewash its walls every summer and clean out its fireplaces every winter. She wanted to live in it until she grew old, forgotten, like some wizened holy man in a cave.

She could never own it, in the same way she could never own existence. She knew that no-one owned anything, not houses, not lovers, not life. Like everything and everyone, like houses and Mademoiselle Joubert and lines of giggling sisters and dogs and the briefest, lightest croissant *au beurre*, her existence was air.

SIXTY-NINE

The love of hands

IN KEEPING WITH THE FAMILY tradition of failing to become great men and women ourselves, instead being history's bit players, my father once got drunk in a bar in a small town in Louisville, Kentucky, with the greatest boxer of the twentieth century, Muhammad Ali.

Muhammad Ali was then not yet a great boxer. He still went by the name of Cassius, which my father believed was Roman, as in Emperor Cassius. He was not a great drinker either, Emperor Cassius. 'He was a two-pot screamer,' said my father. 'He couldn't hold his grog.'

How my father happened to be in the same Louisville bar as Cassius Clay I never found out. My father was everywhere for a while, travelling on his magic carpet, appearing and disappearing in a blink. I do know that as the night wore on Emperor Cassius and my father stole a hat stand from the bar and waltzed it down the street.

'Can you remember anything else? You know, anything he said about civil rights or boxing or religion?'

'Nope,' he said.

Besides waltzing a hat stand down the street the only thing my father recalled was Emperor Cassius asking him to place his hand on the bar. 'He put his hand next to mine,' my father said. 'Maybe he was measuring the difference.'

Ever since I have tried to make out Muhammad Ali's hands in photographs and film clips. The bones of the palms, the four bones of the fingers, the knuckles, the web of tendons and veins beneath the skin, the principal tool of the body to reach out and grasp the world. The first part of the body to be held out in greeting, in friendship, in meeting. In some countries, after a handshake, the palm of the hand is placed against the heart.

The average length of an adult male hand is one hundred and eighty-nine millimetres. Each fingertip holds a dense web of nerve endings.

My father's hands were not of average length, being as small as a girl's. Perhaps Emperor Cassius admired my father's small, defence-less lily-white hands, so useless at catching, so different from his own hands, faster than a striking snake, capable of felling all comers.

Because my own small hands have a tendency to sweat, I have never liked holding hands. I was even anxious about holding hands with my small son. When he was eight my son told me that he no longer wished to hold my worried hand.

My hands hold anger as well as my worries. Once, in a fit of temper, I placed my hands around my adolescent son's neck. Once, in despair, I slapped my small hand across my sister's beautiful face.

Recently I saw footage of Muhammad Ali, reduced to pure body by the end. His mind was elsewhere, his hands calcified, numb, their stories lost to him. His hands were now catchless too, those same hands that once stung like a bee.

SEVENTY

The worried lover

AFTER THE BEAUTIFUL LOVER LEFT for Tunisia, after spring had ended and the Suspicious Wanderer moved out of Horatia's flat into a small studio of her own belonging to an American academic, her life once again fell into a pattern. She noted that even wandering, unclaimed persons crave order, a design to place upon the plotless days.

She didn't walk the streets as much as she used to. For a start she was busier, working in the mornings on numerous proofreading jobs and in the afternoons and evenings teaching the English classes she still ran out of Horatia's sumptuous apartment. She earned enough to pay her rent and to shop every Wednesday and Saturday at the market at the end of her street. She earned enough for an occasional meal and a small *pichet* of wine at a cheap restaurant. On rare instances when she had coffee and a croissant she always stood at the counter instead of sitting down, because it was cheaper, and if she ever went to bars with friends she kept the same drink in her hand throughout the night. Her studio was in the thirteenth arrondissement, near the *périphérique*, in a rundown part of rue Jeanne d'Arc, and she chose it because she liked the name of the street.

By then she was eligible for a much-coveted *carte de séjour*. By then she had heard of AIDS, known in France as SIDA. To get her *carte de séjour* she had to have an AIDS test, to find out whether all that condom-free sex had killed her.

By then all the lovers of the world were crowding in on her. By then, she felt jostled by elbows, torsos, knees. Sometimes the teeth of strangers appeared too close and she imagined she heard the sound of tooth against tooth, as if accidentally knocking teeth when kissing. The thought of opening her mouth to a stranger, of having an unknown tongue swimming against her own, repulsed her. She, who had always loved kissing! The thought of having an unknown penis enter her body struck her as ludicrous, impossible. She was so tired of endless lessons involving the tongue, the hands, the ears, the belly and the fallible heart.

Even though the Suspicious Wanderer tested negative for HIV, she began to imagine that the virus lurked undetected in her blood. Wasn't it possible that it existed, not yet manifested? Wasn't it possible that her body was polluted, that in truth it was a shameful, dark thing, too little loved?

At night all the lovers she had known swam around her head. Leonardo della Francesca, the shadow lover, Stephen Porter, the Scandinavian lover with the too-full lips, the long-lost Nina Payne, the dissolute lover. Had she loved any of them? Had anyone loved her? She remembered that Jonathan Jamieson had loved her, and she had loved him. She remembered that love was supposed to mean desiring the happiness of the lover as much as one desired it for oneself. It meant letting a house or a dress or a person be themselves or itself, without imposing your own wants or desires, without confusing the lover with someone else or with anything they were not. Let the leaf be the leaf, let the dress be the dress, let the lover be himself or herself, unopposed!

Had she been kind enough? Had she listened hard enough or well enough? Oh, too late, too late! She was ready to give herself up to the practice of love just as her body was dying!

She wrote to Ro in Sydney, who wrote back advising her to have another test. *Has anyone ever told you you're a fuckwit?* Ro wrote. *Don't be an idiot, Deb, just have another test. Honestly, you are the most neurotic woman I've ever known. It's lucky I'm fond of you. Here's my diagnosis, free of charge: you haven't got AIDS.*

Steph did not yet know about the Suspicious Wanderer's AIDS hysteria. By chance she wrote to the Suspicious Wanderer to tell her that a mutual friend, Vanessa, a heterosexual woman, had just been diagnosed with HIV. She contracted it during a one-night stand, having sex without a condom.

By the time Ro spoke to Steph, and Steph called the Suspicious Wanderer in Paris, she was nearly out of her mind. 'You do know that Vanessa slept with the man in Zimbabwe, don't you, where half the population carries HIV?' But nothing Steph said could convince the Suspicious Wanderer that she was not dying because, like all irrational fears, they were the hardest to eradicate.

One of Horatia's oldest friends was a distinguished doctor and she introduced him to the Suspicious Wanderer. They liked each other at once, for Bertrand had an outrageous sense of humour which appealed to her, as hers appealed to him. He worked out of a famous teaching hospital, the Pitié-Salpêtrière, and at a dinner party at Horatia's one night she managed to ask him a few questions about AIDS. A gay man himself, with a partner of some thirty-five years, Bertrand was of the opinion that it was a most interesting disease, the progress of which was impossible to predict.

'There will be growth, then decline, *peut-être*,' he said. 'This is *normale*. It will possibly destroy parts of *la population africaine*.'

'How long does it take to manifest itself in the blood?' she asked.

He looked at her, hard. 'Come and see me in my clinic, *ma chère fille*.'

The Pitié-Salpêtrière was a beautiful building, possibly used in earlier days to display the fallen heads of kings and queens. Paris's proud history was beginning to strike her as too proud, too overbearing. She was beginning to hate buildings with a history as long as your arm and starting to think fondly of Australia and its puny buildings with no collective memories.

Bertrand was behind his desk, smoking a cheroot. At least she assumed it was a cheroot because it was not a cigarette. The *ne pas fumer* laws were only just starting to come in, and bars were still full of smokers, with a reserved section at the centre of the bar for non-smokers. She had sometimes stood beside a small *ne pas fumer* sign in a bar, smoking her heart out. 'Death by pleasure,' Bertrand said and smiled at her.

'Sorry,' she said in English. 'The bus was late.' She appeared to have forgotten her French.

'Paris used to be inhabited by citizens,' Bertrand said. 'Now it is an office. Philippe thinks we should move to Algiers.'

She smiled at him. She no longer knew what she was doing there and what it was that had once seemed so urgent to say.

Bertrand did not speak further but continued to smoke. She had seen Frenchmen break for cigarettes between tennis sets, and once she had seen two women smoking in a public swimming pool, their legs and torsos immersed in water, their shoulders and arms resting against the ledge of the pool.

'Think of me as a tin opener, *ma chère fille*,' Bertrand said. 'You cannot tell me anything that will shock me. I already know that the most extraordinary things happen to ordinary people. I know that ordinary people have the most extraordinary lives.'

He offered her a coffee, and when she accepted he picked up a beautiful little bell on his desk, some kind of antique, and rang it. A secretary came in, a middle-aged woman who looked like she might have been a French actress, with a big sultry mouth and hair in her eyes.

'*Pourrais-tu nous apporter un café, s'il te plaît*, Celestine?' he said.

'Thank you so much for seeing me, Bertrand,' the Suspicious Wanderer said when Celestine had left the room. 'I know how busy you are. I know you must have a million and one more urgent things to do. I really appreciate you taking the time to see me. How do you do it? How do you keep yourself sane? All the horrible stories you must come across, dealing with the sick and the dying every day, with the very worst things that can happen. A friend of mine has a brother who's just been diagnosed with multiple sclerosis and another person I know—'

'*Arrêt!* Enough!'

She took a breath. 'Sorry.'

'Don't keep saying sorry. It's—how do you say it?—*irritating*.'

She let out an undignified sound. 'Sorry,' she said, sobbing. 'I'm sorry, I'm sorry.'

Bertrand was very kind. He asked a colleague to join them, a specialist in SIDA. How did she come to be so lucky as to have an expert advising her? Her whole life was a fluke, a chance, preposterously fortunate, as well as clumsy, ruined, made up of failures and blind compulsions.

'Everybody's got one fate,' said Bertrand at one point during that kind hour, as if he was a woman at the village well and not a leading Parisian neurologist. Did neurologists really believe in fate? Did dealing with tragedy every day cause you to throw up your hands, as humbled as the rest?

She left the Pitié-Salpêtrière more composed than when she went in. While she did not entirely believe that she would live, she was willing to entertain the possibility that she might. In her pocket was a note from Celestine. It read: *Au fil des années, les grosses grossissent, les maigres maigrissent, les vieilles vieillissent et meurent. Vous n'êtes pas encore vieux.* As years go by, the fat get fatter, the thin get thinner, the old get older and die. You are not yet old.

Wasn't it a breach of protocol or procedure or privacy for secretaries to slip private messages to patients?

Was she even a patient? She would never, ever work the French out, not even if she lived in France the rest of her life.

SEVENTY-ONE

Roses

BLACK BACCARA, AS DARK AS shiraz, gothic, almost sinister under moonlight. The flower that a witch might chose to give to the beauty.

Albertine, opening out from the curled pink bud into riotous girlishness. Flowering but once a year, a rose that does not behave itself, climbing walls, fences, window frames, its abundant petals dropping carelessly in pink profusion.

Tea roses, yellow, creamy or ivory, barely brushed with colour, hardly perfumed, loved equally by Victorian cottage gardens and by stout matrons and ageing men in sandals and socks.

White, white roses running all around the bower in Sissinghurst's White Garden, as fragrant as spring, spilling above your head, drowning you in perfume. Intoxicating, going straight to the head, making you drunk.

SEVENTY-TWO

The bird lover

HOW SMALL THE WORLD GROWS as the long day closes, how the map shrinks to birds in flight outside the window, to the rush of wind in the trees, to the push of the single bulb through the soil.

The swoop of birds in flight, singing on the wing, a chatter of bells. Rushing by the window, chimes in the wind.

Measuring the days by the poetry of birds, by the bells from the church on the hill. This small world, intimate, domestic. This crowded world, infinite, immense, bounded by the walls of this house, by the unfurling of leaves, by the customary walk to the café by the fountain, where I sit, recalling the days. Everything connected with this body, my personal memories, cancelled with the end of my corporeal existence. My hand on the cup, my feet in their shoes, my breathing heart, remembering.

SEVENTY-THREE

Marché aux puces

SLOWLY THE SUSPICIOUS WANDERER'S IRRATIONAL fears became more rational. Slowly, on the scale between madness and sanity, the hands came to rest at a balanced point, that point recognised by therapists and counsellors and other practitioners of the mind and heart as being a reasonable one from which to practise living. In truth, this accepted scale is often disregarded by the minds and hearts of men and women living according to unwitting impulses. In truth, the mind and heart is often off the scale and only murder, suicide or unlawful acts bring this truth to our attention.

On weekends the Suspicious Wanderer frequented the *marché aux puces*. She noted the detritus of life, the remains, the favourite vases, the baby boots, the photographs. The vanished person captured in the frame, the photograph all that is left after the vanished person and everyone who knew her have left the earth.

She wasn't lonely. There was this world, and the next. There was this world of physical objects and people she loved, croissants and houses and wine and her own feet to hold her up, and a long line of women preceding her, stretching back before disappearing into time's wondrous vanish. She was always accompanied.

Celestine rang her on a Sunday evening after she had been to a market. Her English was as clumsy as the Suspicious Wanderer's French but she managed to make it clear that she was inviting the Suspicious Wanderer to a soirée.

She was going to attend, out of curiosity. She was going to attend, despite the fact that she still couldn't believe Celestine's breach of the rules. How did she get her phone number? And would Bertrand be there?

Celestine's apartment was in a curved building on a corner, so that all its rooms curved too. It was like being in the prow of a ship, except that the beautiful curved windows looked out over a square in an expensive *quartier*. She didn't know anyone in the handsome crowd, expensively attired. Waiters circulated with drinks, and she quickly downed two glasses of champagne. Bertrand and his lover Philippe were in a corner and she waved. Bertrand lifted his glass.

Two women standing nearby were speaking English.

'Are you friends of Celestine's?' she asked when they smiled at her.

'I am,' one of them said. 'Andrea. Pleased to meet you.' The woman held out a hand. She was in her mid-fifties, rich-looking. The Suspicious Wanderer introduced herself; the woman explained that she lived in the apartment directly below Celestine's and introduced her friend, who was visiting from London.

'Amazing building,' said the Suspicious Wanderer.

'Owned by Celestine's father,' said Andrea. 'He owns half of Paris.'

She knew it would be rude to ask why Celestine was working as a secretary. Maybe she wasn't a secretary. Maybe she was a doctor who also happened to serve coffee.

'Where is our hostess?' asked the Suspicious Wanderer.

'Over there,' said Andrea. 'She's just come in.'

Celestine was standing by the door, smoking a cigarette. She looked cross, as if she would rather be somewhere else. She was in a knot of people which included Bertrand and Philippe. The Suspicious Wanderer could not detect any boss–employee body language.

The Suspicious Wanderer was coming out of the bathroom when she ran into Celestine.

'*Vous n'êtes pas mort*,' Celestine said. 'You are not dead.'

'*Évidemment*,' the Suspicious Wanderer replied.

'*Bon*—good.' Celestine smiled and walked off.

The Suspicious Wanderer could not have explained how she found herself in Celestine's bed later that night. It might have been the champagne or the fact that she was in Paris, detached from her former shape, that outline drawn in by her family, her friends, by everything that had previously described her. It might have been the same impulse that caused her to climb into Claudette, that car she loved, with a dissolute lover who had just placed a tab of acid on her tongue. It may even have been a buried longing to close the space between her mother and herself.

Whatever it was, the Suspicious Wanderer felt a little scared and a little embarrassed, but also fabulously brave.

SEVENTY-FOUR

Song of Songs

THE SWOOP OF MY VOICE rising up from my lungs, swelling with song. The 'O' formed by the open mouth, the body opening into joy, making music with the breath, the tongue, the palate, the reeds made of flesh in the throat. Anyone who can speak can sing, anyone with a tongue in their mouth and a heart in their chest.

Singing my heart out in Claudette, the windows wound down, with Steph in the back seat playing her guitar. We sang duets, her soprano dipping in and around my contralto, seamless, unpractised, effortlessly beautiful.

Singing with Steph on a summer's day on the Pont Marie, the song and the bridge and the beauty of the day marrying above our heads, rising to the sky.

The old man singing at the concert in the nursing home just before my mother died. Too frail to stand, sitting collapsed in a chair, balancing on his walking stick. In the history of the world, 'Some Enchanted Evening' never sounded lovelier.

The church choir, soaring, in the sacred dome of the White Chapel in the Tower of London, where a queen went to pray before she lost her head. Was it silent that cold morning or were there remnants of songs caught in the bricks as she prayed?

SEVENTY-FIVE

Celestine

CELESTINE WAS A MYSTERY. CELESTINE was surly lips and a sudden outbreak of laughter, bursting from her, loud, like a bark.

Celestine was dinner for two at Balzar, where, after dinner and cigarettes, every waiter knew to bring her a small glass of a *digestif* made from Normandy apples.

Celestine was Saturday mornings sitting on the sofa with the sun streaming in the curved windows, trying to read *Le Monde* with her feet on your lap. A French singer you have never heard before played on the sound system behind your heads, mournful, low, filling you with happiness.

Celestine was languor personified. She did not appear to have worries, or cares, or problems. If she ever had any, she must have decided long before to shrug them off, so that nothing settled. She resembled Catherine Deneuve in her later years, a less formal version, more disarrayed. Celestine's hair was always in her eyes, there was ash on her blouse, ink on her fingers.

Celestine was mordant wit; 'mordant' from the French *mordre*, to bite. She bit off the heads of shop assistants and anyone she considered foolish. Because she did not often smile, she sometimes appeared forbidding. She often looked cross.

Celestine was a neat, compact body with muscular legs. Every morning she jogged twenty laps around the Jardin du Luxembourg.

Celestine was evenings in bed, not entirely abandoning yourself in her arms. You were too self-conscious, too aware of the strangeness of kissing a woman. Throughout, part of you remained off to one side, observing like an anthropologist the sexual habits of the bisexual French woman. She loved both men and women, youths and maidens.

Celestine was the surprise of finding out what one woman did to another in bed.

SEVENTY-SIX

The legs pumping

THERE IS SOMETHING TO BE said for the legs pumping the pedals of a bicycle, for the thrill running up the ankles, the calves, the thighs. There is something to be said for the feeling of life moving through the body, the press of the powerful muscles of the leg on the downward pedal. I have known the sensation of flying through the air on a bike, my hair streaming, pushing into oxygen.

SEVENTY-SEVEN

A pencil

I AM AN ARTIST OF the fingers, of the hand sweeping across drawing paper, the *shush shush* sound of the edge of the hand shuffling across a page, and the small scratching of a soft lead pencil. I am an artist of the journey between object, eye and hand, of bringing to the page what the eye sees.

What I put on the page is usually a clumsy rendition of what my eye sees. A tree, a chair, a sleeping dog, a passing face, none of it technically correct or rendered well, none of it the work of a trained artist. And yet my eyes and hands have been schooled by life, by the shape of the clouds, by the branches of trees, by the face of my baby son. I drew him sleeping, a milk blister on his upper lip, still part of that great cloud of unknowing, unfurled as a bud. Object lover: a new Faber-Castell 5B pencil, fresh from the shop, the pointed steel-coloured tip emerging from the smooth blond wood. The softest leads make perfect dark lines across the white of the page. Holding a new pencil gently between the thumb and the forefinger and pressing it for the first time against the page.

SEVENTY-EIGHT

Brasserie Balzar

IN TAKING UP WITH CELESTINE, the Suspicious Wanderer was granted entrance to the set behind the film that was Paris.

She discovered curious things, such as the fact that the average Parisian married at around twenty-two and had two point five children by twenty-five, which possibly accounted for all the beautifully dressed young families she saw about the place. Unlike her own country, unlike England and America, where women supposedly kept one ear cocked to the ticking of their biological clocks and at the age of thirty-five rushed off in a panic to have a baby, French women calmly birthed their babies while their flesh was still firm, before going off to a clinic to have their cellulite dealt with and their bodies massaged. All the while, rich or poor, pregnant or not, they still flirted expertly with men as if they had never heard of feminism, as if Simone de Beauvoir had never existed.

Even behind the film, Paris still maintained its mysteries. It was a mystery seeing Celestine at a party full of young things, her chic abandoned, clicking her fingers to that embarrassing French idea of a rock star, Johnny Hallyday. All the young men and women dancing to Johnny were conservatively dressed and worked as accountants or as civil servants (*fonctionnaires*). What had happened to the *soixante-huiters* who plucked the cobbled stones from the streets to hurl at police? Where were the artists to *épater le bourgeois*? The young danced old-fashioned rock-and-roll-style too, with partners, as if they were at a 1956 high school dance wearing bobby socks and petticoats. '*C'est le roc,*' said Celestine, snapping her fingers.

Parisians always took their holidays in the same place, year in, year out. They worked only the hours they were required to work, eating lunch cheaply on government and employer-sponsored meal tickets, and then retired on fat pensions. They poked fun at low-browed peasants from Normandy, at funny-accented folk from Languedoc and at *les rosbifs*. Unlike the English, who still made tired convict jokes about Australians, the French regarded Australians as impossibly exotic, marooned in a faraway Gauguin-coloured land peopled by tigers and brightly coloured parrots. Celestine took to calling the Suspicious Wanderer '*mon petit kangourou*' and unveiled a secret wish to visit *la roche rouge*.

The Suspicious Wanderer wouldn't live with Celestine. For a start, it turned out she was impossibly rich, amusing herself with a job as Bertrand's assistant (although a real secretary did the actual work). Her surname included a 'de', which meant she was born into that class which lost its collective head in the revolution. She was a *soixante-huiter* herself, and still had Communist Party associations. She had given a lot of money to various causes but the cause most dear to her was Médecins Sans Frontières. In this, Celestine was not a dilettante; she had worked in Sudan and the Côte d'Ivoire, managing the administerial set-up of bases for field workers, and she still worked as a volunteer one day a week in the MSF headquarters in a street off rue de la Roquette.

The Suspicious Wanderer was scrupulous about paying half for everything, which meant they couldn't eat out as much as Celestine would have liked. One blue spring evening, after the Suspicious Wanderer had saved up for a dinner at Balzar and they had finished their meal, they sat outside on the pavement with their coffees and *digestifs*. The Suspicious Wanderer retrieved from her purse her carefully saved fifty-franc note, placing it under the saucer of her coffee cup in advance of the bill. Just as she did so a man raced up, snatched it, and ran off down the street. The Suspicious Wanderer and Celestine looked at each other open-mouthed.

At the same moment an ageing waiter happened to be emerging with the bill. He shook his head. '*Les pauvres sont toujours avec nous,*' he said sadly.

'*Ils ne devraient pas être,*' Celestine replied.

He screwed up the bill.

'What did you say?' the Suspicious Wanderer asked Celestine.

'I told him the poor should not always be with us, as he suggests. We are rich enough to have no poor.'

The ancient waiter bought them another two *digestifs*, to steady their nerves. He refused to accept payment.

The Suspicious Wanderer enjoyed being marooned outside language. While she still studied French, and her comprehension skills improved and she could more easily read *Le Monde* without a dictionary, she could never quite remember the structure of a French sentence. She always spoke in the present tense, for example, and often spoke French sentences as if they were English ones. Frequently the subjects and the verbs of her sentences were completely askew, so that she sounded like an unschooled four-year-old, or an idiot. She noticed that not completely understanding what people were talking about was oddly restful. You could dream in peace and imagine every conversation was full of wit or significance.

With Celestine she travelled to the Vendée, to the family holiday house at Brétignolles sur Mer where Celestine had spent every summer of her life. For days they lay dazed on sand as crunchy as raw sugar, walking naked and brown around the old stone house and out into the garden. They lay in the chilly arms of the Atlantic and, later, in the warm seductions of the Mediterranean off Corsica.

She was with Celestine one late spring day when she met the man she knew she would marry. The knowledge came to her body first, a sensation that felt like intuition, a knowingness, a feeling of great calm and certainty. At the same time she experienced a rush, a tilt of the earth, much like the feeling that followed the first drag on a cigarette when she had not smoked for some time. Sounds came to her abnormally clearly: a motorbike backfiring, a man shouting out the price of vegetables, the scrape of a café chair against cement. The spring air was spicy, fresh, she distinguished coffee, croissants, the smell of the Seine. They were sitting in a café not far from the river. It was a Saturday, and a passing bride in a simple satin sheath dress was holding a posy of ivory roses. The Suspicious Wanderer looked at her future husband, and her future husband looked back, and everything they needed to know about each other passed between them.

She had not been practising romance all her life for nothing.

The bath lover

HOW COULD I FORGET THE poetry of the bath? The limbs collapsing, swimming, cupped warm and safe, the skin and nerves and fibres of the heart surrounded once again by comforting water, as warm as amniotic fluid.

That delicious equation

AND MASSAGES. THE BODY WORKED upon like clay, like dough, reduced to sinew, muscle, pulp. Each part of the body individually tended to, taken apart: the torso, the muscles of the back, the limbs, each leg, each arm, the hands, the feet, the scalp, the face. The secret moment of transformation, that delicious equation, when the body usurps the head. The organs of the body turned to soup: the urethra, the kidneys, the liver, the heart. The hands and feet forgetting to sweat, the brain and its thoughts finally disarmed, the conscious self reduced to pure body. Is the self the physical body? Or is the body the vessel for the self? On the massage table, the self is only a body.

EIGHTY-ONE

Coup de foudre—The princely lover

FOR EVERYONE SAFE FROM WAR, injustice, plagues and starvation, the choice of who to love becomes the most important question of existence. If you are not in chains or interned in the Doge's Palace, everything of value rests on your choice: where you live, what you hope for, how joyful or sad your life will be. Work and love, is there anything else? What picture of life is found in your lover's face? What future is seen there?

My future husband had horizons in his face. He had freedom in his eyes, dreams, hopes, infinite opportunities in his fingertips. I looked at him and my future appeared, dazzling, more beautiful than I could have believed.

I saw boats on shining seas, a house of laughing children. I saw rooms of people I wanted to know, swooping movement, a big life. I saw a man I recognised at once.

'*Coup de foudre*. Love at first sight.' I heard Celestine say, a voice through cloud.

I turned my eyes from him and looked at Celestine, who I had forgotten. 'Deborah, *je te présente mon ami* David. David, *voici* Deborah.'

He had the same name as my father.

EIGHTY-TWO

Prince

OUR DAYS WERE GLAD.

Our days were counted not in the number of breaths that we took but in the number of moments that took our breath away.

We counted ourselves lucky.

We counted out the hours we had left to us, each of us set like clocks, with our handful of seconds.

We counted the colours and sounds and smells of the world, saturated with detail.

He was a lawyer, did I tell you that? He had a job, shoes, clothes, by which I mean to say that he was of the world, a real person, as well as the man of my dreams.

He was English and he lived on a houseboat on the Seine, a converted freight transporter with creaking floors, moored opposite the Petit Palais.

He was a lawyer but a lawyer with a heart (insert jokes here). He worked for Médecins Sans Frontières.

He spoke flawless French.

His father was a famous children's book illustrator, an artist. His father was a member of the British Academy and belonged to the Chelsea Arts Club, a place I had always wanted to go.

How fast a person can move from a standing position! How quickly a person can go from being loveless to being loved! Within seconds of laying eyes on my prince, my life rearranged itself into a miraculous new pattern, a shape yet to be revealed to me but which I already knew contained everything I wanted.

But first things first: over Celestine's head, the man of my dreams asked me to meet him later that same afternoon.

'But I don't even know you!' I said, laughing.

'Yes, you do,' he said.

He told me where his houseboat was moored, with explicit instructions on how to distinguish his boat, *Scheherazade*, from the rest. I was watching his mouth move: his bottom teeth were slightly crooked. His front teeth, the teeth he smiled with, were straight and white.

What can I tell you about his face? He had blue eyes, arrestingly blue, a smallish mouth, a slight cleft in the middle of his chin as if a child's finger had pushed itself into clay. It was an intelligent face, sensitive, passable as handsome. He wore his brown hair long, tangled and curled round his ears, the nape of his neck. It was a face that you might pass in the street without a second glance, but for me it was a specific face in which I could read the future.

I noticed he was tall. I noticed his body had a natural grace and that he moved with ease. He had beautiful hands.

'Je suis ici, mon petit kangourou,' said poor Celestine, who might as well have been a scarf slipped unnoticed from the back of a chair to the floor. When I turned my eyes towards her it took me a moment to recognise who she was. *'Deborah?'*

Had I ever seen her eyes look so worried?

Had I ever properly looked at her before?

Walking home, Celestine, uncharacteristically, talked all the way. She chattered on like a schoolgirl, about this and that, about our plans for the weekend. All I wanted to hear her speak about was him.

'How long have you known him?' I asked.

For a moment it appeared she was going to answer 'Who?' but I could see the struggle and its aftermath, the sad news settling in her face. I saw that her face was not sultry at all but full of suffering.

'Several years,' she said. 'Much longer than you, *évidemment.'*

We walked on, past our favourite florist, with flowers arranged like living works of art, arranged as only Parisians could arrange flowers, with every detail perfect, each arrangement as beautiful as a painting. I wanted to gather up armfuls of beauty, to eat it, to become the flowers. I wanted to arrest the moment, to stay dazed and smote all the days of my life.

EIGHTY-THREE

The tree lover

SOMETIMES YOU HAVE TO DO nothing except lie on your back with your eyes closed, preferably with your bare toes touching grass. Sometimes you have to lie on a picnic rug, anywhere near a spreading tree, and open your eyes to look up into the spreading tree, a living green umbrella. Any tree will do, but ideally one with arms that embrace you, reaching out and around you, a dome of branches and leaves. The great oaks of Richmond Park, where you can lie close to the descendants of deer brought there by a king escaping the London plague. The chestnuts of France, with their blossoms like artfully designed cakes scattered like decorations in a Christmas tree. The strangler figs of Queensland, with their whiskery, old-man beards, and their cousins, Moreton Bay figs, rigged like boats, a fretwork of sinewy branches twisting and turning, as tangled as ropes. Sometimes you have to cry at the beauty of a single cherry tree in blossom, of the white stars strung like lights, so white against the perfect blue of the sky. I lay upon the earth one spring and looked up at such a tree and my heart sang because it knew what it meant to be beating.

EIGHTY-FOUR

Toes

THERE IS NOTHING LIKE IT: mudflats at low tide, the slivers of silver water, the ooze between the toes, the adult feet returned to childhood, shoes off, crab holes everywhere and, if you are lucky, a cloud of crabs with their bony, articulated limbs swarming across the ruffled mud.

EIGHTY-FIVE

A black pearl

MY FATHER ONCE BROUGHT ME back a gleaming black pearl. He flew in on his magic carpet from a land of lotus leaves and burning candles and there it was: a glistening drop of beauty on a silver chain.

My father selected only me for this pearl: not my beautiful mother, and not my beautiful sister Jane. 'It goes with your skin,' he said, doing up the clasp at the back of my neck. The black pearl sat perfectly in the scoop of my collarbone as if all my life my bones had been waiting for its touch.

EIGHTY-SIX

David, David, David

EVERYONE WARNED US ABOUT GETTING married so soon. On the telephone from Australia Ro said, 'You're getting *what*? Wasn't it you who made the jokes about "better dead than wed"?' Steph and I had the first and only falling-out of our friendship: she sent a postcard of her heroine, Emma Goldman, scrawled with a quote: 'On rare occasions one does hear of a miraculous case of a married couple falling in love after marriage, but on close examination it will be found that it is a mere adjustment to the inevitable.' Beneath it, she wrote, 'Deb, why not have the honeymoon without the wedding? Why not wait to see if you like him first? It doesn't sound like a good idea to me, marrying someone you've known for three weeks.'

I replied, in writing trembling with emotion, 'How dare you, Steph! Never in a million years would I advise you not to get married, or not to have a baby, or to have one. That's between you and Nasser. These decisions are intimate, deep, personal, the most private decisions any of us can make. I would never offer you my opinion on such a thing and I'm shocked that you would.' I later learnt that after reading this Steph rushed around to Ro's tiny house in Balmain, sobbing.

Celestine said: 'Why rush? He will still be there in six months. If he loves you, he will still be there in a year.'

She began a campaign to win me back, to sanity if not to her arms. She took me to the opera, to a house on the cliffs of Normandy for a weekend, to a private soirée at the Hôtel de Marigny. She took me to a ball at a chateau near Fontainebleau, a ball that lasted till dawn, with baccarat tables and jazz bands in rooms with gilded ceilings, rock bands in tents in the gardens, peacocks on the lawns, waiters moving along hallways that resembled Versailles' golden passages, painted, mirrored, dazzling. There were real peasants staring through the locked fences as we drove in. 'Celestine, you secret aristocrat,' I said. She laughed, wound down her window, and shouted, *'Liberté, égalité, fraternité!'* The peasants cheered.

Horatia said: 'You are like a child who wants to eat up all the ice-cream in the world. Being grown-up means stopping before you make yourself sick.'

I replied: 'Thank you, Dr Freud. I didn't know you were an expert on these matters.'

She looked at me and smiled. 'Well, my dear, I can see that your mind is already made up. When you want something, you really want it, don't you?'

I really wanted my dream lover.

I really wanted my perfect lover, my prince, having waited and waited.

I really wanted to hand myself up, as if on a plate, a liver, a heart, dissected for his delectation.

I really wanted to eat up all the ice-cream in the world until I was sick.

I really wanted to die in his arms, just like in a fairytale, going up, incandescent.

I saw that in choosing him I was closing the door on that intimate room in which Ro and Steph and I had dwelt so long, that cosy room in which we told each other secrets about men who loved bottoms and lovers who fell in love with desire and soft-eyed Arab boys who wore silk cravats. I knew I had to join that world of responsible emotional engagement before I was lost, stranded forever on the shores of adolescence, where girlish intimacies stood in for adult intimacies between women and men. I had never before burdened myself with the responsibilities of a mutual adult relationship.

We rushed, laughing, him and me, down the rue de Rivoli to buy the golden rings inscribed with our names.

We rushed, love at our heels, flying to our future.

I was wearing the orangey-red dress I was in love with, holding the hand of my perfect lover, arrived at last.

We were married in the Mairie du quatrième, just us, with no-one else present. I wore a lace top I had found at a *marché aux puces*, which I dyed by leaving it in a bowl of tea overnight.

Our first night married we washed each other's bodies, tenderly, the palms of each other's hands, the soles of each other's feet. With a soft cloth and a bowl of warm water we anointed each other.

Afterwards we lay in each other's arms on his creaking boat and all the happiness of the world came to rest upon our heads. We felt a kind of religious beatitude.

EIGHTY-SEVEN

The unrequited lover

THERE HAS TO BE ONE unrequited love in a life.

My unrequited lover was romantic love, which naturally and properly never gave me what it promised, exposing me as a child who believed she was growing up to turn into a swan.

EIGHTY-EIGHT

Horatia

HORATIA LIVED THROUGH THE SECOND World War. She was in the army, the ATS, and wore a soldier's khaki uniform. She once showed me a picture of herself in it, a pretty girl with a Veronica Lake hairstyle swept over one eye.

Horatia was a driver. For a time she drove a general around a bomb-struck London and he was so impressed with her that she was recruited to the team who looked after the prime minister.

Sometimes she took out Clementine (that is, Mrs Churchill) for a secret night drive around the blackened streets. Clementine referred to Horatia as her 'blue-eyed girl' and sat in the back, rarely talking. Horatia said that these speechless night drives sometimes return to her now in her old age: the city without lights, driving in blackness, hardly recognising what she was seeing.

Horatia drove Winston Churchill and King George VI up from London to the wilds of North Yorkshire on a secret visit to inspect the preparations for D-Day. The army was using a beautiful twelfth-century Augustinian priory as a training site. When they arrived troops were scrambling all over the medieval walls, practising on them in preparation for the ruined stones of northern France.

Horatia did not know that she was witnessing preparations for the biggest invading force the world had ever seen. All she remembers is that on the way up the king asked Churchill for a cigar. And Churchill had very dirty fingernails. 'I'd have hated to sit next to him at dinner,' she said. 'They were enough to put you off your food.'

Horatia, history's bit player like the rest. Horatia, that cleverest of women, not clever enough to know history when she fell over it. Horatia knew Churchill was the prime minister, of course, and that the king was the king, but all the while as she was driving them north she was thinking only of her heart, broken at the time, and how she couldn't give a fig for anything but the lover who had deceived her.

My new husband and I lay in our floating honeymoon bed, while above our heads a spaceship reached Neptune and in Berlin the statues of Lenin came down. The world was roaring but we were deaf, dumb and blind to everything but each other's breathing faces.

EIGHTY-NINE

Gelato

I RECOMMEND EATING AN ITALIAN GELATO, freshly made so that it dissolves upon the tongue, a cascade of sugar and fruit and happiness. Eat standing up on ancient stones, surrounded by Florentine housewives lugging their shopping and schoolchildren shouting at each other. Eat it so you can marvel at the creaminess, the sugar content expertly balanced, mixed with air. Originally made from ice and snow brought down from the mountains, gelato eaten on a honeymoon rail trip from Paris to Florence, via Milan, tastes like love.

NINETY

Breath

EVERY NOW AND THEN YOU have to stop and acknowledge that you are breathing. Notice the rise and fall of your chest, the inhalation and exhalation of your breath, the faint vibration of your beating heart. Notice sounds coming to your ears (birdsong, the distant sound of traffic, a tractor in a field close by). Notice the smells of early morning: coffee, toast, the lovely scent of fresh earth washed by overnight dew. Can you stop and smell the world, hear it in your ears, feel the breath in your body? Can you send up a prayer of thankfulness, to God or whoever or whatever is responsible for the creation of yourself and your moment of breath? So soon breathless, we come breathing and we leave stilled. Count your blessings, count your breaths, each individual breath invisibly inscribed with a number.

NINETY-ONE

Australia

ROMANCE BETWEEN THE AVERAGE COUPLE dies two years, six months and twenty-five days into marriage.

Romance might be said to have died between my new husband and me earlier than statistics suggest. Precisely one year, two months and twelve days into our marriage, when he came home from work to our leaking boat and found me still sitting in the same clothes I was wearing when he left (my pyjamas), our new baby son screaming in my lap, surrounded by the scattered pages of the book I was supposed to be editing. 'Christ,' he remarked, before turning and walking away.

'Christ,' he said again when he came home three hours later. 'What's the matter with you?'

I was tempted to say 'Everything' but I did not.

I cried. I have noticed that most men do not enjoy it when women cry, especially dishevelled women sitting in their pyjamas with screaming babies in their laps.

'Why do you turn everything into such a drama?' he said. 'You'd think you were the first woman in the world to have a baby!'

I cried harder.

'I'm sick of this,' he said, which I noticed was his most common expression.

'I want to go home,' I said, when I could stop crying long enough to speak.

He laughed. 'There's no way on God's earth I'm going to live in Australia.'

We cried on and on, my baby son and me, that baby boy who arrived unplanned and already in love with me, believing my body to be as bountiful as a fruiting tree, my breasts as bountiful as an ocean.

'I want to go home,' I said again two days later, when I was dressed and sitting upright, my back against a banquette in La Tartine, a watered-down glass of Côte du Rhone in front of me. The baby was staying with the Portuguese concierge in Celestine's building, who cooed and clucked over him all the hours he was awake.

'I thought you wanted to live in Paris forever,' my husband said.

'That was before I had a baby,' I said.

'Do you want him to turn out like an Aussie bloke? Graceless and charmless?'

'Yes,' I said. 'I mean no. Not all Australian men are graceless and charmless. You're as bad as Horatia.'

He snorted. 'Horatia.' My husband had taken an instant dislike to Horatia. 'A spoilt princess' is how he described her, a woman so insecure she surrounded herself with acolytes who worshipped her.

'Look,' I said, 'you've never been to Australia. How would you know what it's like?'

He smiled. 'Do I have to hang myself to know what being hanged is like?'

'That's ridiculous.'

'Is it?'

We glared at each other.

'Well, I'm going to go home for a while,' I said. 'I want my family to meet the baby.'

My husband did not like my family either. My parents had recently visited us in Paris, and my husband had booked a table at Chez Julien—a table perilously close to a posh couple from England who spoke with upper-class accents reeking of Eton, army officers' messes and the Chelsea Flower Show. Before long my drunken father was loudly mimicking their accents, while my drunken mother laughed uproariously at his wit.

'Ah, the jumped-up white trash that is your family,' he said.

How quickly we travelled from sacred love to sacrilege.

For the record, arranged marriages have just as much chance of turning into lasting happiness as love matches. And, remarkably, marriages between couples who have known each other only three weeks have as much chance of success as marriages between couples who have known each other for years. This is a statistic based on a survey of four thousand couples by a prestigious American family research institute.

For the record, we started out with as much chance as anyone. We wished to be bound together forever. We wanted to dissolve into each other, for our marriage to be a shared skin. Our motives were pure: I wished everything for him, everything good. I wanted to be perfect for him, a universe in one body, mother, daughter, God. Like my forebear Rose, I wanted to look only at my husband.

Let me put it another way: I still believed I was going to turn into a swan.

Back in Australia I showed our son the Australian sky, which blazed at night with the points of the Southern Cross, wider and larger and emptier than the French sky. We listened to the laughs of kookaburras and I showed him the frills, as stiff as Elizabethan collars, around the necks of startled lizards. I showed him his own toes in ruffled mudflats at low tide as well as bearded fig trees which took up the sky. I showed him his first Australian beach washed by the Pacific Ocean while his fat starfish hands held fast to the strap of my bathers as we held our laughing heads above the frothing waves.

·

My sister was away in New York, working as a personal assistant to a famous model, being shouted at and living in the same apartment block as the model. 'She loves it,' said my mother, whose turban was slightly askew.

My brother Paul came to see us but he was drunk and I wouldn't let him hold the baby.

'What do ya think I'm gunna do? Drop it?'

'Yes,' I said, holding the baby tighter.

'Aw, piss off,' he said, stomping off. He slammed the front door.

'When did he start speaking like that?' I asked my mother.

'If you lie down with dogs you get up with fleas,' said my father, who had come into the room. 'Drink?'

'No thanks, I'm breastfeeding,' I said.

'It'll knock the little tyke out for the night,' said my father, pouring me one anyway. In truth, I did drink, but only occasionally and never more than one watered-down glass of wine.

I was thinking of my absent husband, and what he would think of my brother, whom he had yet to meet.

I looked down at my son, at his beautiful sleeping face. He looked so much like his father that all the love I had for my husband came flooding back and I wanted nothing more than for the three of us to be together again on our rocking boat, Paris around our heads.

NINETY-TWO

Duck

I FORGOT TO TELL YOU about my son's birth. How the streets of Paris shone in the early-morning light outside the window of the American Hospital at Neuilly, how he shot out, a screaming blue boy, and how my husband laughed, his face elated. Afterwards, in my private room with a mini-bar, we opened a bottle of icy-cold Veuve and inspected the menu options, which resembled a restaurant menu, including the chef's daily speciality. *'Je vais prendre le confit de canard,'* I said. I was drunk with joy, in love with our future, which stretched out waiting to be filled. Don't think I didn't know I was lucky.

Three days after we got home to *Scheherazade* a new friend from one of the other permanent moorings urged us to go out for a celebration dinner. She was Italian, with grown-up children, dying to get her hands on the new baby.

'But he'll need a feed,' I protested.

Somehow, between the combined exhortations of Paola and my husband, I found myself dressed, with breast pads in my nursing bra, heading for La Tour d'Argent.

We sat at a table by the window, amid the silver and the damask, eating pressed duck we could ill afford. The Belle Époque ceilings and walls floated with clouds, the wine played upon our tongues, my breasts leaked milky tears. Our duck had its own number, and afterwards the waiter gave us a postcard with our duck's number printed on it, which pictured the same cloudy blue room in which Russian czars and kings had also eaten slaughtered ducks.

'Thank you, darling,' said my husband, raising his glass. 'You are the most beautiful mother in the world. Here's to you.'

I raised my glass to his. 'Here's to us.'

We smiled at each other.

NINETY-THREE

The first lover I slept with after I lost my husband

HOW LONG DOES IT TAKE to love properly? Now I am old enough to know the difference between being in love and loving someone, to know that the eating-up-all-the-ice-cream-in-the-world euphoria passes, and that in some lucky cases romance is replaced with a deep nurturing attachment, as tangled and wide as the feeling between parent and child, or between sisters.

I still think of my husband as my husband, even though he is my sister's husband now. I wonder if they fell in love at once, like we did. If they did, I was too busy to notice at the time. I was looking the other way, an absent-minded witness, only comprehending everything backwards.

I wonder if when romance between them died it evolved into a deep nurturing bond, if they are now like two old geese on the Seine, mated for life.

They still live aboard *Scheherazade*. My sister sleeps in my former bed, in that creaking cabin, her breath mixing with my husband's breath. It is the same cabin to which we brought home our baby son, where the three of us slept together for the first time on earth.

I have heard that their daughter looks like him. As far as I know, my son has never met his half-sister or, if he has, he certainly would not tell me.

Sometimes, as if in a dream, I recall the incident of the broken mirror, towards the end of our marriage. Without warning the old mirror above the sink in the bathroom aboard *Scheherazade* suddenly fell into the sink and smashed. My husband said he would buy a new one and that afternoon, when I returned to the boat with our son, I saw that a new mirror was in place above the sink.

I stood in the corridor outside the bathroom and saw immediately that the new mirror had been positioned too high. When I stood directly in front of it, I could only just see the hair on the very top of my head.

'It's too high,' I said. 'I can't see my face.'

'You don't need to,' my husband said. 'I'm the one who has to shave every day. It's always been too low for me.'

As in a dream, the story of the mirror tells the story of our marriage, each of us struggling to see ourselves, the mirror forever too high or too low, never reflecting our mutual faces.

The first lover I slept with after I lost my husband was a kind man. He waited a long time for me, longer than most hopeful lovers would wait. I was deep in a cave of ice, and it was impossible for me to imagine myself thawed. By then I could not see myself in any mirror on earth, but one night the kind lover traced his careful fingers slowly around my necklace of sultanas and I heard the first crack.

NINETY-FOUR

Hotel sheets

THE NIGHT MY MOTHER DIED, before I lost my husband, the world was silent. It was as if it grieved for her, and wished to match the stillness of her breath.

My sister and I were with her as she left the world, the last time we three were together. We watched her go, caught the moment life left her body, flying away. Life was breath, and when breath was gone my sister and I walked out motherless into the stillness of the world. The night was cloudless, the stars ablaze, and for the moment I could not feel the hatred for my mother that had been part of me for so long, a blood memory. I was suddenly wretched, abandoned, and my sister Jane and I turned to each other under the brilliant night sky, and sobbed.

We were staying together at a motel. Our father had not long moved into the aged-care home which had for several years housed our mother. My father flirted with the women who served his meals and his tongue still desired his evening drink of three parts overproof rum and one part Coke. The night our mother died he was in his bed, after falling asleep, drunk. Our brother Paul was long in his grave.

I remember the drive back to the motel. It resembled the long, flickering dreamlike drive through deserted streets the rainy night my sister was born: the earth suddenly silent, the flimsy fabric between the past and the future ripped asunder, the body's radar picking up every sound, sensation and smell of a strange new world. We didn't speak and as we turned into the motel, the first pearly light came into the sky.

There was only a double bed in the room. We were so exhausted that we brushed our teeth before stripping down to our underwear and getting into bed.

'I love crisp white hotel sheets against my body,' said Jane.

'Me too,' I said. 'I love the smell, and the feel.'

She backed into me, so that we were spooned like an old married couple. 'Cuddle me, sis,' said my beautiful sister.

I put my arm around her slender waist and snuggled into her warm back. She put her hand around my arm. 'I love you, Debs,' she said, raising my hand to kiss it.

I sometimes wonder if, like me, she remembers.

NINETY-FIVE

Another house as object lover

I LOVED THIS HOUSE AS soon as I saw it. I loved its outline, its shape, its crooked roof and low front door. I loved that it was two hundred and seventy years old, older than the first European-built house in Australia. I loved the huge crusty oven set into its bricks and the cellar, the well in the garden, its many windows opened in welcome to the church bells ringing out the hours. I loved its old shutters and its ancient stone walls and straight away I wanted to know the stories of every single person who had lived in it. If I have settled anywhere upon the earth, it is here.

In this part of southern France, spring agricultural fairs are common. The Master of the Cassoulet brings out his robes, the Mistress of the Cheese, the Commander of Flour, all dressed as if in mayoral finery, with sashes and ribbons and heavy medallions hanging from golden chains. Great long tables are set up in communal halls, or beneath marquees on the grass, and huge cauldrons of stews or cavalcades of sausages are dished out to communards. In my village every spring there is also a procession of tractors, huge shiny new red ones, as big as fire engines, and little ancient machines from the early twentieth century, trundling along with enormous wheels like old-fashioned prams. The farmers sitting on the tractors tip their hats or wave, and we who line the streets wave back. Everyone knows we are saluting animals, grass, wheat, rain, air, soil and the sun, every living thing that brings us our existence.

I take back ripe spilling mature cheeses to my house. I take back wine and bread and cuts of meat that my butcher proffers tenderly, cradling them as carefully as if they were a new baby. I take back the proud new shoots of asparagus, which the asparagus seller makes sure I know how to cook. He looks dubious about selling perfect new-season asparagus to me, someone he mistakes for a *rosbif*, who might murder it in its moment of glory. I take all these things and make a meal from them, sitting in the dissolving present moment in a tended garden of apple trees, rhododendrons, lavender, scarlet geraniums and early spring roses. I live as if everything that happens to me is a magnificent afterlife.

I own this house because of the Sydney property boom of the late twentieth century, which magically turned the ordinary house where I grew up into a goldmine, transforming my father and mother into well-off people. When they died my sister and I inherited enough money to buy, respectively, a studio flat at Bondi Beach for my sister to use during her infrequent visits to Australia and a ramshackle house in France for me, for which I feel both grateful and obscurely guilty.

The money I have left over supplements my modest editing income, as well as my son's desire to study at Saint Martins in London. My husband's father is still alive, ninety-two and still painting and drawing, and our son lives with his grandfather in a beautiful house in St John's Wood. A sensitive boy, my son learnt long ago not to talk to me about his father, and never to mention my sister's name. Of course I am ashamed of this, but I was born preferring death to surrender. Like my parents before me, I am the possessor of violent emotions.

Where I have chosen to live is close enough to London for my son to visit. I pick him up in my old banger from Carcassonne airport, now on the airline budget route from Stansted. I wait for him in the flimsy terminal as pale English tourists are disgorged, together with befuddled locals, and then the face of my adored, newly adult son, that face more dear to me than any face I know.

I keep a room for him. He is a young man of grace and charm, half-English, half-Australian, a French speaker, his heritage to be forever torn between north and south, a lover of northern-hemisphere seasons and southern-hemisphere skies, with roots reaching out in all directions. Like me, he loves freezing Christmases and sweltering Christmases, his exiled heart schooled to pursue what is beyond.

NINETY-SIX

The deathly lover

SHE DOES NOT LIKE TO think of her brother. She hates to think of him, in fact, breathless, stopped, that boy who once dragged a reluctant dog across a polished floor.

Steph told her that her brother was no less real even though she could no longer see him, just as Russia was no less real even though she couldn't see it.

Steph advised her to adopt the Gestalt technique of speaking out loud, saying carefully and clearly: 'I choose to have a brother who is dead.'

She tried it, but only once.

The words in the air sounded so bleak, so bare, so awful, that she rushed from the room, leaving them behind, running and running.

She does not like to think of all the things she did not do: go to him, hold his hand, drag him screaming to some faraway place to stop him drinking himself to death. She does not like to think of her own culpability.

What happened to those years between him rising from the bed and getting into that car? How did she come to not know her own brother?

The guilty truth is that the woman did not see her brother Paul often. One time she did not see him for three years straight, when he was in the Northern Territory working and she was in Paris, grieving. He lost his driver's licence in Gove, where he was working at the mines, for drink driving. He was jailed in Darwin for driving a mate's car while drunk. It was these years that turned out to be crucial, the years when it might still have been possible to reach out and save him. But as he was going down she was looking the other way, and she did not know what was approaching.

She has a bag which contains all his worldly possessions: a jumper with holes, smelling of cigarettes and of him; a fraying wallet; a couple of old vinyl records (*Harvest*, which they used to play over and over); and an old torn photograph of all of them at the beach in Queensland, her brother, her sister and herself, still children, their parents standing behind them, much taller than their children, more beautiful and more glamorous than they could possibly hope to be.

Paul, Ro, Super Nan, her mother and father, citizens of that vast republic of the dead. Nana Elsie, stilled.

Where have they gone, the pictures inside Nana Elsie's head of dancing around a room with a handsome captain? What of the pictures inside Paul's head, and Ro's, and that picture in her mother's head of holding a knife against a daughter's soft throat?

Where will her own pictures go? Who but she apprehends the world with her particular eyes, grasping it with her ten particular fingers and ten particular toes? What body but hers bears these unique scars, the story of a life made manifest? No self without a body, no body without a remembering self to animate it.

The woman who now lives alone in a cottage in southern France is careful to catalogue her body's memories. In the urge to tidy up, to sort through her body's archaeology, she makes sure that pictures pass from head to head, a collective remembering. Her son remembers a sixteen-year-old blind girl growing watercress on a flannel during a long sea crossing in order to have something fresh to eat. He carries a picture of Mademoiselle Joubert, too, adrift in the Australian bush, the daughter of a baker from Angers. As well as inheriting his grandfather's small, girlish hands, her son has also inherited the sound of Aggie thwacking her stick, together with the sound of six sisters, giggling, the youngest one frightened of bushrangers.

But he will never remember his mother longing to kiss the lips of Justine Gervais. He will never recall how her stomach lurched whenever she saw that dissolute lover, as if she were travelling too fast in a car over an unexpected hill.

These memories will vanish along with her body, lost to the far place that holds the memories of that vast republic.

But while she still breathes, nothing is lost, forgotten or forgiven. While she still breathes the past is permanent, unredeemed, and the present dissolving, slipping away. Oh, to be capable of smelling ripe cheeses and roses! What it is to be breathing!

NINETY-SEVEN

Rain

ON THE FACE, THE EYES closed, head back, upturned. Water trickling into the coiled ear, round the back of the hair, down the neck. Standing naked in the garden, before anyone is up, not even an animal. The rain against your shoulders, your breasts, your belly, your grateful face, making the soil dance around your feet.

NINETY-EIGHT

Scheherazade

EVERYBODY KNEW BUT ME. PAOLA knew, and Celestine knew and, unforgivably, Horatia, because Celestine told her. Why didn't anyone tell me? I never spoke to any of them again.

I spoke to my sister only once after I found out. Rather, I *screamed* at my sister only once. I can still hear the sound of that scream, as if it hangs permanently somewhere in the air.

In despair, I slapped my small hand across my sister's beautiful face.

'Don't you dare give me that bullshit,' I said. 'You sound like you're in a B-grade movie.'

'He doesn't love you anymore,' she said.

I laughed. 'He doesn't mind sleeping with me.' I clenched and unclenched my fists.

'Look at you,' she said, in a sneering voice that sounded like our mother's. 'You always think you'll get exactly what you want, don't you?'

'Get out,' I said loudly. 'Get off this boat now.'

'Gladly,' she said. 'He hasn't loved you for a long time, you know. He said he didn't realise what love was until he met me.'

I rushed at her; she raised her hands in self-protection. 'Tell me while you have the chance, Jane,' I said, breathing hard into her face and holding her by the hair. 'Do you really want him or do you only want to win him from me?'

She giggled and I slapped her again.

'Mama,' said my son, walking in, 'are you wrestling?'

'Yes,' I said. 'Mama is wrestling with Aunty Jane. Now go back to your room, sweetheart.'

Jane lunged for the door, bolting up the stairs to the deck. *Scheherazade* rocked on the water.

I sometimes wonder what would have happened if my son had not come in, how far my violent emotions might have taken me.

Not long after this we left *Scheherazade* forever. I was sadder to be leaving her than to be leaving my husband, whom I had not loved, not deeply and not properly, for some time. If I still loved him at all, I loved the memory of him, of what he and I had been and what we might have become. I loved his most pure self, which I believed I glimpsed when we were first in love. It was him I grieved for, that man who once wanted only good things for me and for our coming child.

I thought I grieved most keenly for the loss of *Scheherazade*, for the community of permanent boat-owners: Russian heiresses and adventurers, shifty men from Margate, former shopkeepers from Turin. I could not stand the loss of the river in the morning in mid-winter, a white mist coming off the rippled surface of the water. I grieved for our summer life, sipping wine in chairs on the deck, the smell of potted lavender and thyme and basil baking in the sun. Most of all I mourned the loss of the rock and sway of life on the water, for the passing of my sea legs, for the taking away of that joyous sensation of being warm and dry, loved, afloat, which I believed I would never feel again.

NINETY-NINE

The second-last lover

A SUSPICIOUS WANDERER WHO HAS spent her life wandering, flitting from here to there, from house to house, from flat to boat, looking for love in cities and villages, in endless places and faces, might count herself surprised to find that love came when she wasn't looking. Surely she had learnt that history begins and ends unnoticed and that when an inconsequential action tilts everything in an unheard-of direction men and women are most often looking elsewhere.

Love arrived smaller and more humble than advertised. Love turned out to be plain, quotidian. Love was many encompassing things, painful, conflicted. It was more terrible than publicised.

Love was in the room when her son was in his hospital bed in London, his body rigged up to machines. She would have cut it out then, exorcised it from her breathing heart, but she could not.

Her son did not die but came home to recuperate and she was still suspicious of love.

She saw her lost husband once, from behind. He looked stooped, sad, walking along the hospital corridor, and she was more surprised than she could say to feel her heart swell with a tender feeling that resembled forgiveness.

Love was in the ground, in the old stones of the house, in the scarlet geraniums around her door and in the pillow placed against her lower back by her old friend Steph, who came to stay when she slipped on the ice and broke her ribs.

Love did not really stretch to forgiveness. Not for Jane or Horatia or Paola. It probably did not stretch to her husband either, now that she thought about it.

Love was a nuisance. It meant considering other people besides oneself, a difficult adjustment for a temperamental, deeply solitary person to make. In truth she did not enjoy having to consider other people.

Love was Phillip, that unprepossessing English handyman who lived two houses up. Bald, too fat, with bad English teeth and a riotous laugh, he loved red wine, the French, driving all over France and Italy even though he could barely read a map. He loved life, really loved it, the gift of eyes, of ears, of a flowering tongue with which to taste everything it offered. He dug in the earth's soil and knew the name of every bird and tree, and thought nothing of fixing for free the broken window of old Madame Morel so that she could remove the black plastic she had taped across it and once again look out over the valley. Love was the two deep lines running down each side of his face, where happiness had carved itself.

The Suspicious Wanderer had grown fat too. Her belly flopped over the waistband of her skirts and if she had once, long ago, possessed graceful ballerina legs, she did not now. She had grey in her hair and yellowing teeth and a couple of scars that she might tell you about if she had knocked back a few too many happy glasses of *vin de pays*.

Sex with Phillip was a bit of a laugh. They prodded each other's fat bellies with their fingers.

'Watch it,' he said once. 'Thirty years ago I was out of your league. Thirty years ago I was a god.'

She laughed. 'Thirty years ago I wouldn't have looked twice at you either,' she replied.

And she wouldn't have. She preferred herself now, less succulent and more loving, humbled, loved.

THE HUNDREDTH LOVER

TICK-TOCK. TICK-TOCK, the body remembers. A human lifespan is less than a thousand months long, really, just a single gleaming day.

My body, mine at last.

I am wearing a red shirt.

I was here, an ordinary citizen of the sated world and nothing exceptional ever happened to me, save the commonplace and extraordinary fact that, like you, I was born, I was born, I was born.

C'est la vie, so thrilling, so terrible, that I stand before it, hope-lessly ardent, saluting before I forget. Every day unique in its details, already passing, vanishing, like breath.

Acknowledgements

THIS BOOK HAS HAD A long gestation. I would firstly like to thank the fantastic team at Allen & Unwin for their patience and understanding, most especially Annette Barlow. Patrick Gallagher was always supportive and the editorial team of Christa Munns and the brilliant editor Ali Lavau saved me from my worst excesses. My long-time former agent, Margaret Connolly, encouraged me through thick and thin, and I'd like to thank her and her husband Jamie Grant for many years of unflinching support. My friends Sandra Hogan and Emma Felton continue to be the anchors of my life, as do their husbands Danny Troy and Kevin Hayes, who have become my dear friends too. My mother Barbara Johnson, and my brothers Steven and Ian, and their wives Janet and Michelle, continue to be rock solid, and I thank them. My sons, Caspar and Elliot Webb, provided much-needed distraction. I'd also like to thank everyone in BrisVegas who helped our coming home during a difficult time; in particular, the brilliant author and editor

Matthew Condon, who changed my life in giving me my lovely job at *Qweekend* at *The Courier-Mail*. Thanks, too, to David Fagan and Michael Crutcher and to my fab colleagues Sandra Killen, Leisa Scott, Frances Whiting, Anne-Marie Lyons, Phil Stafford, Alison Walsh, Amanda Watt, Matthew Fynes-Clinton, Trent Dalton, Mike Colman, Russell Shakespeare, David Kelly, Genevieve Faulkner and everyone else on that mighty team. BrisVegas locals are some of the friendliest and most generous people on the planet: big thanks to Rob Hugall and Issy Hugall and Meg Hinchcliffe; Chris Strew; Kristina Olsson; Janet and Bob England; Cathy Jenkins; Rosa Hogan and Annette Hogan; Chris Whitelaw and John Hook; Paul Reynolds, Ross Booker and the fine team at Education Queensland, including the unstoppable Lyn McKenzie; Cameron Belcher and Jennifer Brasher; Donna Wright; Joan Wilson-Jones; Maria Comninos; Susan Oakenfull and Ian Oakenfull; Judy McLennan; Robyn Flynn; Billy and Nikki Webb and everybody in Sydney and Melbourne who were there too, including Anna, Maddy-Rose and Tom MacClulich, Tracey Callander, Leigh Hobbs, Dmetri Kakmi, Jim Pavlidis, Megan Backhouse, Ross Tanner and Elizabeth Minter, all of whom helped make the transition from London to Brisbane easier for me and the boys. *Merci* Marion Cabanes for helping with my French. Special thanks to JH, who knows what for.